Assassins Of The Dead 2
Dragon Touched

Assassins Of The Dead 2
Dragon Touched

Avril Sabine

Cracked Acorn Productions
Australia

Assassins Of The Dead 2: Dragon Touched

Published by

Cracked Acorn Productions

PO Box 1365

Gympie, Queensland 4570

Australia

978-1-925617-11-5 (Kindle)

978-1-925617-12-2 (EPUB)

978-1-925617-13-9 (Print)

978-1-925941-38-8 (Printed In Australia)

Genre: Young Adult Fantasy/Paranormal

Copyright 2017 © Avril Sabine

Cover design by Caitlyn Petersen

For all my children.
Not just the ones I gave birth to.

Some heroes work in the shadows, only their deeds remembered.

Meikah, Kellan, Livia and Rafe travel to the Arcton Mountains when an assassin comes asking for help. A vampire holding is overrun by zombies. But it's not the bandits and necromancers that most fear in the area. It's the dragons and their nesting grounds. Cross a dragon and they never forget. And certainly never forgive. In an area known for its myths, legends and dangers you need to stay vigilant if you want to survive.

*

This story was written by an Australian author using Australian spelling.

Name Pronunciation

Like many names there is more than one way to pronounce the following ones. These are the pronunciations used in this story.

Amiel (ah-meel)

Breena (bree-nah)

Ena (en-ah)

Isha (ee-sha)

Kellan (kell-en)

Letha (lee-thah)

Livia (liv-ee-ah)

Magan (mag-en)

Maksim (mack-sim)

Meikah (mee-cah)

Naren (nah-wren)

Sarette (sah-ret)

Suri (sue-ree)

Urian (you-ree-en)

Chapter One

Meikah crouched beside Rafe, trying to find Kellan in the shadows. She spotted him crossing the area between the hedge they crouched behind and the tree they were headed towards. "I can't do that." Maybe if they wore their dark clothes and mask that made it easy to hide in the shadows, she would have a better chance reaching the tree undetected.

"Want me to carry you?" Rafe asked. "I can move just as quickly with you in my arms."

"How did I let Kellan talk me into this? We should have started with something simpler." She tried not to think about the chemise Kellan carried, folded up and tucked into a dark, cloth bag. "The Duke will throw us in prison."

"Kellan seems to think he won't." Rafe peered past her. "He's reached the tree. Do you want me to carry you?"

She leaned forward. It didn't help. "Are you sure he's there?"

"My senses are better than a human's."

She still didn't know much about vampires. But Rafe didn't seem like the typical ones most of the stories spoke about. She'd only ever seen him feed on one unwilling victim and she didn't know if she could call him a victim since he'd been attacking them at the time.

"Are you going? Kellan is signalling you."

She took a deep breath. Remaining crouched in the shadows wasn't going to stop the rumours about her being a necromancer. They might be true, to an extent, but she wasn't the kind of necromancer they thought she was. "Can you see the guards?"

"If you take the same path Kellan took, you'll avoid being seen by them."

She looked between the tree and Rafe. Should she tell him she had no idea what path Kellan had taken? She looked down at her dark trousers and shirt, which didn't seem to blend into the shadows as well as the Assassins Of The Dead gear. A pity she didn't have her night blades and the mask they wore when doing missions. "This isn't going to end well."

"You agreed."

"It was probably from the relief of capturing

Magan and surviving her creatures." If they'd been able to go last night, like they'd planned, maybe she wouldn't have spent all day thinking about the things that could go wrong.

"Kellan is signalling you again."

"All right. I'm going." She tried to see where the guards were. It was impossible. There were too many shadows in the castle gardens. Her stomach lurched at the reminder of where she was. Kellan was crazy. Which didn't say much about her own sanity since she'd agreed with the plan.

She inched forward, reluctantly leaving the shelter of the hedge. Keeping low she glanced around as she crept towards the tree. It felt like a hundred eyes watched her, waiting to pounce. If she was lucky, it was only two pairs. A crunch sounded beneath her foot and she realised she'd left the paved path and stepped onto the edge of a garden bed. She froze, holding her breath as she listened. The place was a maze. Who needed a garden with meandering paths, randomly placed flowerbeds and a handful of lanterns and lampposts with bewitched flames? They should have put in straight paths, more hedges and lots of trees. Or anything that would have created plenty of shadows.

Nothing seemed to move and she heard no sounds.

Easing back from the garden bed, she crept along the path. Her breath sounded loud in the night, her heart faster than it should be. The tree slowly came closer. Far too slowly. She kicked a pebble that was on the path, wincing as it skittered away from her.

"Is someone there?"

She froze at the guard's demand. Did he really expect her to answer him? Again she held her breath, barely wanting to blink in case someone noticed the movement. She spotted him, cautiously walking towards her, holding up a lantern with a bewitched flame. Livia's ability to put out the light from a distance would have come in handy.

The light came closer, sweeping over the area off to her right. Not having any choice, she moved slightly, freezing again when the guard swung the light in her direction. He came directly towards her and she feared he'd spotted her.

The light went out and the guard cursed. A rush of air came towards Meikah and she was scooped up, pressed against the hard planes of Rafe's chest, the breeze against her face as she was carried to the tree.

Rafe placed her on the ground in the shadows behind the tree. "I told you to follow the path Kellan took."

Rafe remained close so she was able to clearly hear

his whispered words. "I couldn't see the path he took." She turned to Kellan. "Did you put the lantern out?"

"Yes."

"I really have to learn how to do that."

"It's part of learning how to make your own bewitched flames." Kellan stepped away from her. "Come on. Not far to go now."

"Maybe we should do something else." She moved closer to the tree when the guard relit his lantern.

Kellan chuckled softly. "Too late now. We'd be caught for sure trying to get out of here." He took hold of her hand. "This rumour will have the gossips talking for weeks." He lightly squeezed her hand, continuing to hold it.

"It's not the gossips I'm worried about," she muttered.

Kellan let go of her hand. "This way. Before the other guard returns on his rounds."

She watched Kellan slip away, disappearing into the shadows within seconds. How was she meant to follow him when it was impossible to see where he was going?

"Do you want me to carry you again?" Rafe asked.

She nearly said no. What kind of an assassin couldn't blend with the shadows? But she supposed she'd only decided yesterday that she'd join them. She tried not to remind herself Rafe had joined the day before her. "How do you hide in the shadows? I need to figure out how it's done."

"You'll have to ask a human. My ability to blend with the dark is a vampire power." Rafe placed a hand at her back. "Do you need help?"

She stared up at him, a darker shadow against the night. Could he see her clearly? "Yes." She'd barely spoken the word before she was in his arms and pressed against his chest.

He lowered his head. "Tonight is more interesting than I expected it to be."

Before she could say anything, they were across the garden in a rush of air, her feet on the ground, Rafe's arms around her as she tried to gain her balance. She stepped away. "Thank you."

"It was my pleasure," Rafe said.

Kellan joined them, his head start not having helped him arrive at the location first. "The flag pole is over there." He turned Meikah in the right direction. "See it?"

"The area is full of lights. We'll be caught before we reach it." She eyed the pole, the Duke's flag flying from the top, proclaiming to everyone that he was in residence. The background of the flag consisted of two panels of equal size, the left white and the right red. The silhouette of a winged hound, a forepaw raised, was in the middle of the flag, taking up half the space.

"As soon as the guard begins his rounds we have about seven minutes until the next one reaches a location where he'll be able to see us. More than enough time to take down the flag and hoist the chemise in its place." Kellan chuckled. "This has to be one of my best ideas yet."

That wasn't exactly what she would have called it. "More like your biggest insanity ever."

"The guard is moving," Rafe said.

"Give him time to get out of view." Kellan stepped in front of Meikah. "Run for the pole the moment I start." He looked towards Rafe. "But don't get ahead of me. We wouldn't want to be caught before we're ready to be."

There it was. The part she dreaded. Being caught by the Duke on his nightly walk through the gardens. The time was random each night and they'd watched and waited, hoping the start of his walk fell in with the regular rounds of the guards. They'd got lucky. Or at least that's what Kellan had tried to tell her. She wasn't so sure.

"Now." Kellan ran towards the flagpole, Rafe directly behind him.

Meikah followed, her reactions nowhere near as fast as a vampire's. Kellan was pulling down the flag by the time she reached the pole.

"Get the chemise out of the bag." Kellan nodded to the bag he'd placed on the ground beside the pole.

Meikah picked it up, pulling the garment out of the bag, freezing when she heard a voice behind her.

"The rumours of swimming in the fountain, the night before, weren't enough for the week?"

Chapter Two

Meikah spun to see who spoke, her mouth gaping when she saw it was the Duke, the chemise falling from her hands to flutter to the ground. The first thing she noticed was his broad shoulders and muscular build that made him look very much the warrior. Next was his black hair and equally dark eyes. Lastly it was his expression that gave nothing away. Exactly how much trouble had Kellan got them into?

Kellan dropped the flag he'd been holding. "Evening, Your Grace. How did you hear about that so quickly?"

"Your mother came to me today and apologised for your behaviour."

Kellan laughed. "At least tomorrow when she apologises it'll be for something I did."

The Duke nodded towards Meikah and Rafe who

remained frozen at Kellan's side. "Are you going to introduce me to your accomplices?"

Meikah wished once again that her face was covered by the mask they wore for their missions. She should have known she'd end up in more trouble than necessary. Letting Kellan do all the planning had obviously been a bad idea.

Kellan gestured to each of them in turn. "Rafe. Meikah."

"Ah, the previous night's compatriots in your fictional swim. Or were you planning on making it a reality tonight? The Duchess asked me to inform you, if I should happen across you, that she will not tolerate anyone swimming in her fountain and believes it might be worthwhile punishing the lot of you to discourage others."

"We have no plans to swim in her fountain and of course if the Duchess feels the need to punish us, we'll accept whatever she decides."

Meikah wanted to throw a bolt of lightning at Kellan before he could get them into more trouble. The only problem was that she had no idea how to do that. She was lucky if she managed to make it crawl along the blades of her weapons when she was fighting spirits.

"How were you planning to be discovered for this

latest prank?" The Duke gestured towards the chemise that lay at Meikah's feet.

"If you'd waited a few more minutes, Your Grace, you would have caught us trying to escape after we'd completed the deed," Kellan said.

"Should I come back in a few minutes? Would that be more suitable for you?" the Duke asked dryly.

Kellan grinned. "That'd never work. The guards you probably have following you at a discrete distance would never believe you let us complete the job."

"I'm guessing you have another plan ready to put into place."

Kellan slowly walked around the Duke. "I was thinking it'd be rude of you not to look in my direction while we're talking. And if I was to move so your back was to the flagpole it would give my companions time to finish the job."

Meikah shared a look with Rafe who shrugged. Surely the Duke wasn't going to let them get away with the prank.

The Duke kept turning as Kellan continued to move. "One of my guards is likely to come forward. Have you thought of that?"

"Of course they will, but by then, the new flag will

have been hoisted and they'll be able to say they saw it flying."

Rafe stepped closer, so he could whisper in Meikah's ear. "I think he's serious."

"I'm afraid he is too." Meikah bent to tie the chemise to the rope. "Get ready to hoist it."

"Your companions are taking their time," the Duke said.

Kellan shrugged. "They're new to this."

"Leading them astray, Kellan?"

Kellan chuckled. "So it would appear."

"Your Grace." A guard hurried forward, pointing towards the chemise Rafe was hoisting aloft.

The Duke turned and stared at the new flag. "Who are you trying to tell the people is currently in residence? Hopefully it isn't the Duchess. I fear she'd be most upset."

"Maybe it's the ladies who are in residence. No one in particular of course, Your Grace," Kellan said.

Meikah moved closer to Rafe, not sure what she should do. How could Kellan remain so calm? She wanted to run and never show her face in Dreyton again. She could almost hear the prison door clanging shut.

The Duke gestured the guard forward. "Swap the 'flags' and make sure you give Kellan his 'flag'. He'll want to wear it tomorrow when he carries my flag through the town. It is obvious he needs to learn what the flag looks like."

Meikah finally found her voice. He wasn't going to throw them in prison? "What about us, Your Grace?"

"This is a warning. If you continue to follow Kellan on his escapades you'll join him for any future punishments."

Kellan took the chemise the guard held out to him, his grin not faltering. "It's all right. I take full responsibility for this prank. They tried to talk me out of it. I obviously don't listen."

Meikah drew in a deep breath, straightening her shoulders as she met the Duke's gaze, clasping her hands behind her back so no one would notice the tremble in them. "Your Grace, I'll walk with Kellan tomorrow and help him carry the flag." She wanted the rumours to fly. Hiding at home wouldn't get that done. She didn't want to have to go through this again any time too soon. It had been a lot worse than she'd expected.

The Duke looked towards Rafe. "And you? Will you join them too?"

"Only if you allow me to do so in a chained coffin, Your Grace."

The Duke inclined his head. "That will be

sufficient. I wouldn't want you killed over the matter. I'll expect the three of you here tomorrow morning at eight." With one last nod towards them, he walked away, the guard remaining at his side.

Meikah waited until the Duke had moved out of sight before she spoke. "How could you talk to him like that?" It had taken all her courage to speak a couple of polite sentences. Kellan had done more than that.

"I've known him my entire life. He gave me pastries when I was a child and my mother told me no more or I'd be sick." Kellan laughed softly. "He'd wait until her back was turned, wink and say it'd be our secret before he gave me two."

"But-" She looked in the direction the Duke had gone. "He's…" She had no idea what to say. All her life her family had talked about the Duke like he was the most important person in the world. The one who could change their lives for good or bad. Her stomach lurched. What if she'd caused him to rethink letting her grandfather be on the council?

"Are you all right?" Kellan reached for her.

She stepped away before he could make contact. "We should go." What had she been thinking? She should have started small and worked her way up to a prank this big. If her family threw her out, when they learned what she'd done, she wouldn't blame them.

"Ready to go home?" Kellan returned the chemise to the cloth bag.

"I was ready to go home before we arrived," Meikah said.

Kellan draped an arm around her shoulders, doing the same to Rafe, who momentarily looked startled. "Wait until tomorrow. The gossips are going to be in their element."

"What are you planning?"

Kellan chuckled. "I wouldn't want to ruin the surprise." He looked towards Rafe as they started forward. "I'll ask Mace to drive the wagon for you. He'll make certain no one does anything to your coffin."

"Should I not have offered to join your parade through the streets?" Rafe asked.

"It'll be all right," Kellan said. "There will always be people who hate vampires and want to get rid of you. But you're one of us now. We won't let that happen."

"Does Danton take everyone in?" Meikah asked.

"No. Between him and Amiel they seem to know who to welcome and who to turn away," Kellan said.

Chapter Three

A figure came out of the shadows wearing a hooded jacket, startling Meikah.

Kellan reached for his sword at the same time as Rafe drew back. He seemed to become one with the nearby shadows, a bat streaking forward to circle around them. The bat landed nearby, becoming Rafe. He lifted his arms up to stare at his forearms, turning them to check both sides.

"That's new." Mace pushed back his hood. "Better than being greeted by a dagger."

Rafe ran a hand over his left forearm. "I've never been able to do that before."

Kellan let go of the hilt of his sword, turning his attention from Rafe to Mace. "Is there a problem?"

Mace dragged his gaze from Rafe. "You're all needed at the bookshop."

"Urgently?" Kellan asked.

Mace shook his head, again looking at Rafe.

"What's going on?" Kellan walked towards the castle gates that they'd been heading for before Mace had arrived.

Surely the Duke hadn't said something to Danton about what they'd done. Had he sent a messenger to complain about them? Meikah glanced at the bag Kellan carried. She didn't want to get Danton in trouble with his brother.

"Another assassin knocked on the door. Showed me his medallion and asked me to fetch Danton." Mace walked at Kellan's side.

Meikah looked behind to check that Rafe followed. Seeing he still looked dazed she dropped back to walk with him. "Are you all right?" She half listened to Mace tell Kellan he had no idea what was going on. The assassin had insisted on talking to Danton alone.

"I don't know." Rafe again looked at his arms. "I haven't done anything different. Not since I joined the assassins."

"We can go over everything and see if we can figure it out," Meikah said.

Mace looked over his shoulder. "Ask Livia. She's a true shapeshifter. Maybe she'll know something."

Rafe stopped.

Meikah turned to face him, coming to a stop too. "What's wrong?"

Rafe slowly shook his head. "It can't be that simple."

"What can't be?" Meikah asked.

Rafe glanced around the area. "Later. When we're alone."

Meikah grinned. His comment brought to mind the moment he'd told her he had her scent and could easily track her. "Another threat?"

Rafe chuckled, looking more himself. "Definitely a promise." He began walking again, catching up with Mace and Kellan. "Do you normally have assassins turn up on your doorstep?"

Mace nodded.

Kellan shrugged. "Sometimes. But they don't usually ask to speak to Danton alone." He walked faster. "Anyone up for a run?"

Meikah groaned. "In the dark?"

Kellan laughed. "Once we step out the castle gates it's straight down the main road to the shop. Worried I'll beat you?"

"You forgot to mention how many blocks that is." She glanced towards him before her gaze was drawn to the gates ahead of them. "Are you serious?"

"Of course I am." Kellan nodded towards the guards as he walked past them.

"Want me to carry you?" Rafe asked. "We could be there before them."

"Really?" She looked Rafe up and down. "I mean, I know you're stronger than a human, but that's a long way."

Rafe scooped her up the moment they stepped through the gates, racing down the road.

The air rushed at her face and she clung to his wiry body, pressed against his chest. Closing her eyes against the sting of the wind, she turned her face towards him, the breeze tugging strands of hair from her plait. "Rafe, put me down. There's no need–" Her words ended abruptly when he stopped in front of the bookshop.

Rafe continued to hold her. "Do you still doubt me?"

She caught a glimpse of fire in his dark eyes. "I never doubted you. I don't know a lot about vampires." When he continued to hold her, she pressed a hand against his chest. There was no beat of a heart and she stared at her hand.

"Is something wrong?"

She shook her head, removing her hand from his chest. "Put me down, Rafe."

He lowered her to the doorstep. "There is something wrong. I heard the beat of your heart change and your breath catch."

"I didn't know vampires have no heartbeat." She tried to read his expression and failed. "It surprised me. You don't seem dead." Nothing like the other dead she'd come across. Spirits that could be shattered into shards of light that quickly disappeared and zombies in various stages of decay.

Rafe started to reach for her, lowering his hand halfway through the action. "That bothers you?"

She stared at him for a moment. "No."

Kellan and Mace ran towards them, laughter proceeding them, Kellan accusing Mace of cheating.

Mace reached them first. "These are the ones who cheated." He gestured towards Rafe and Meikah.

"I'm slow compared to some," Rafe said.

"Really?" Meikah tried not to wince when the word escaped. "I couldn't imagine anyone would be faster than you."

Rafe moved closer to her. "You thought that?"

Kellan brushed past them. "Let's find out what's going on." He stepped inside Fable, Mace following him.

When Meikah would have entered the shop, Rafe

drew her back. "Don't you want to find out what's going on?" she asked.

His gaze roamed her face before his lips slowly curved upwards. "Thank you for allowing me to join you tonight. It was interesting."

"You might end up in a lot of trouble because of it."

Rafe closed the space between them. "You would care?"

She pressed her hand against his chest. "I don't want either of you in trouble because of me."

He took a step back, his gaze going past her. "They're arguing."

Meikah strode inside, stopping when she saw the stranger on the other side of the counter with Danton. He was dressed in leather and dark cloth, a navy so dark it was nearly black. The upper half of his face was covered by a mask, the lower half shaved. The Assassins Of The Dead medallion had been left to hang against the supple leather armour that covered his shirt. Meikah counted at least four daggers and wouldn't have been surprised if there were more. She felt Rafe at her shoulder, close enough he was almost touching.

The man broke off mid sentence to look in their direction, his hand resting on one of his daggers.

After looking her up and down he faced Danton. "Are they all children?"

"We're not children," Livia snarled.

Meikah had been about to say the same words the shapeshifter had spoken.

"You came seeking my help." Danton's voice remained mild, his stance relaxed.

Meikah saw that everyone except Amiel, the necromancer spirit, was in the shop. Shade remained in the curtained doorway behind the counter while Livia, Mace and Kellan were on the same side of the counter as her, looking like they might leap over it.

"I was told you'd help anyone," the man said.

"Only those worthy," Danton said. "Unless you tell me what the problem is and who needs help I can't tell you if it's possible for us to help you."

"You'd be better off asking him how many others have turned him down." Livia's hand remained on her dagger. "I say we show him the door." When Danton made a motion with his hand Livia remained silent, resorting to glaring at the man.

"You were the one who came to my door, at this late hour, asking for help. Don't expect me to offer the help of my people until I know what you want them to do, including the risks they will face." Danton paused a moment, meeting the man's gaze.

"None of them are children. They're all adults regardless of how young some of them look." He glanced at Kellan. "Or act."

Mace elbowed Kellan. "He was talking about you."

"I'm sure he was looking at you," Kellan said.

Chapter Four

Meikah was tempted to smile at Mace and Kellan's antics, but was worried about what the assassin wanted. Danton might look relaxed, and Amiel nowhere to be seen, but that didn't mean anything. Danton always appeared relaxed.

The man faced Kellan and Mace. "Do you think this is a joke? Lives are at stake. An entire village is overrun by zombies."

"A bit like Dreyton yesterday morning," Mace said.

Kellan nodded. "Until we dealt with the problem."

"You don't understand the gravity of the situation," the man said.

"Which town?" Danton asked.

The man faced him. "Longview."

Rafe stepped past Meikah. "That's a vampire holding."

"I didn't know they had Assassins Of The Dead there," Livia said.

"They don't. We're at King's Peak, but patrol the entire mountains."

"They wouldn't help you because it was a vampire holding?" Rafe asked.

"We are only a small group and the mountains are a large area. Most of our group isn't due back for weeks. The other groups I approached have their own problems to deal with." The man paused a moment. "Only one suggested I shouldn't worry since they're vampires."

"You will send a report to the capital." Danton's voice was firm, no question in the words. "Headquarters needs to know about the refusal."

The man nodded. "That attitude isn't what we're about."

"What have you been doing about the problem?" Danton asked.

"I left my partner behind to try and relocate the townspeople, but there aren't many places they can go. Not that are suitable for vampires." The man glanced around the shop. "It's too much for a group of young adults to deal with." He stressed the word young.

Danton looked to Kellan. "You and Mace can go tomorrow."

"There might be a slight problem with that," Kellan said.

Danton looked from Kellan to Mace, his gaze remaining on Mace. "You didn't arrive in time to stop the prank."

Mace shrugged. "I guess not. I met them on the way out."

"What happened?" Danton listened patiently to Kellan's brief explanation.

The man gestured towards Kellan. "This is who you would have help us? A prankster."

Meikah began to protest, Kellan interrupted her. "If you don't want people to focus on something, it's necessary to direct their attention elsewhere."

"With a prank."

Meikah could understand the disbelief she could hear in the assassin's voice. It had taken time for her to be convinced too.

"I want to go with you," Rafe said. "There might be something I can do to help."

Danton shook his head. "If too many of us left at once people would notice and wonder what was going on."

Kellan grinned. "Not if we had a reason to leave."

"I haven't agreed to let you help," the man said.

Mace and Kellan shared a look before both chuckled. Kellan faced the man. "You think you could prevent us? Assassins Of The Dead are welcome wherever there's a need." He drew out his medallion. "I can show mine around as easily as you can show yours."

Danton interrupted the man, who'd started to speak again. "What is your plan, Kellan?"

"The Duchess can send us on a task as a punishment for swimming in her fountain."

"Not Meikah. She hasn't had enough training," Danton said.

She strode forward to stand at Kellan's side. "I fought with you yesterday morning. I risked my life to save Webb and to defeat Magan. I'm going."

"I'm going too," Livia said. "I'm not going to be left behind when there are more interesting things happening."

"We always fight together," Shade said.

"Not always," Livia said.

"Nearly always."

Danton held up a hand and they fell silent. "You can't all go. Some of you need to remain and guard Dreyton with me."

Voices rose in argument. The man shook his head. "This group will be useless."

Shade reached under the counter and drew out a piece of parchment he separated into three, writing 'stay' on two and 'go' on one. He folded them and cupped his hand around them, holding his hands out to Livia.

She stepped back, pointing to Mace. "He can draw first."

Mace shared a look with Kellan who nodded. Stepping up to the counter, Mace drew a piece of parchment from Shade's cupped hands, unfolding it. "Stay."

Livia drew one out. "Go." She grinned. "I'm going."

Shade dropped the third piece of parchment on the counter and took hold of her hand. "You will be careful. Return to me in one piece." Twisters danced in his eyes, the wind swirling back and forth.

"I wish we could all go," Livia said.

"So I can go?" Meikah asked.

"No," Danton said at the same time as Kellan said, "Yes."

Danton shook his head. "She's not ready. She's had no training."

"For people to believe it's a punishment the three of us have to go," Kellan said.

Rafe moved to the other side of Meikah. "We won't let her come to harm." He grinned, canine teeth appearing. "You should be more worried about those who might come against Meikah." Flames appeared in his eyes.

The man stared at Rafe. "A vampire necromancer? I didn't think it was possible."

Rafe shrugged, not answering.

"What would the Duchess send you for that would take you away from Dreyton for possibly weeks?" Danton asked.

"King's Peak are famed for their silk scarves," Kellan said.

Mace nodded. "That sounds like something she'd want."

"A single silk scarf?" Meikah wasn't sure anyone would believe that excuse.

"A trinket we have to go to great lengths and inconvenience to acquire. It's the ideal task." Kellan turned to the assassin, holding out his hand. "I'm Kellan."

The assassin stared at Kellan's hand for a moment before he took it. "Flint."

They each came forward and introduced

themselves, shaking Flint's hand. Shade was last. "Do you need to take any supplies back with you?"

Flint shook his head. "Supplies aren't a problem. It's being unable to venture out of doors that's the problem. If things go on too long then we'll have to worry about supplies."

"Do you know who's sending the zombies? Or why?" Livia asked.

"The mountains go for miles. It could be anyone, anywhere. It doesn't help that necromancers tend to flee to the Arcton Mountains when they're run out of a town."

"I'll send word to the Duke in the morning." Danton turned to Flint. "If you want somewhere to sleep the night you can stay upstairs. The door on the right at the far end of the hallway. If you're hungry help yourself to whatever you like in the kitchen." He gestured towards the curtained doorway.

Flint nodded. "My thanks. I haven't eaten since late afternoon."

"This way." Danton stepped through the curtained doorway, Flint following him.

Meikah stared after them. "How can Danton be sure he's an assassin? He could have stolen the medallion."

"He would have asked him the code."

Meikah grinned at Kellan's words. "I bet he didn't say it was don't get caught."

Kellan chuckled. "You never know."

Livia smiled at Kellan's words. "I know. Unlike some, I was here when he arrived. He asked for Danton specifically. Said he'd been in the capital a couple of years ago and had heard stories about him."

"What sort of stories?" Meikah asked.

"That he tends to get the job done."

"That doesn't surprise me," Kellan said.

Livia yawned. "I'm turning in for the night." She grinned. "I wouldn't want to miss tomorrow morning's parade."

Kellan returned her grin. "It's going to be an event to remember."

Chapter Five

Meikah saw a mist form in Kellan's clear brown eyes, obscuring the colour. She didn't doubt him. He tended to go out of his way to make sure people talked. "I need to go home. I've got a feeling tomorrow is going to be a long day."

"It might be long, but it's definitely going to be fun." Kellan stepped forward to take Meikah's hand. "I'll walk you home and reset the wards for you."

"Night." Livia strode through the curtained doorway, Shade following Livia after saying goodnight, Mace doing the same.

"I'll walk with you too," Rafe said.

Meikah drew her hand from Kellan's. "I wonder what it's like in the Arcton Mountains." She stepped outside, Rafe and Kellan following her.

"If half the rumours are true it'll be a lawless place filled with myths, legends and danger," Kellan said.

Meikah smiled. "Myths like the Assassins Of The Dead?"

Rafe spoke before Kellan could. "Other myths too. Ones about necromancers, dragon touched, people who disappear without trace, bandits who've hidden treasure they haven't been able to reclaim and creatures that have no name and leave a trail of death behind them."

Meikah glanced at Rafe, not sure if she should believe him. "What sort of creatures?"

"No one knows."

Kellan chuckled. "That only means no one has caught them. Which isn't surprising with the size of the mountains. And that's also why people disappear without a trace. You go off the road and there's a good chance you'll get lost and never find your way home. Unless you're good at tracking and can find your way out again."

"We won't need to go off the roads, will we?" Meikah was beginning to rethink her insistence on going. It had sounded like an adventure and she'd never travelled anywhere before.

Kellan shrugged, the action clear in the light from the street lamp they passed, the bewitched flame steady. "We won't know what to expect until we arrive. Anything is possible." He grinned. "Except getting lost. We'll have Livia and Rafe with us. They'll be able to smell our way out of the mountains."

Reaching her house, Meikah led the way around the back. "I'll see you in the morning." She kept her voice soft, not wanting to wake anyone. Looking up, she noticed light shining out her window. "Oh." She hadn't left a candle burning.

"What's wrong?" Rafe asked.

"I think I'm about to get into trouble." Her gaze remained on her window as she tried to see who might be inside. "It looks like someone's in my room." And the only person likely to be in her room at nearly midnight was one of her parents.

"I'll check for you." Rafe was on the roof and crossing to the window in a blur of motion. He was back equally as fast. "Both your parents. Your mother is sitting on the bed, occasionally shaking her head and your father is pacing back and forth."

It was worse than she'd expected. "That doesn't sound good." She couldn't drag her gaze from the window.

"You can stay at Fable tonight," Kellan suggested.

She was extremely tempted. Nearly said yes. "I better get this over and done with. I'll go in the front door. At least they won't be certain how I got out. I don't want them putting bars on my window." She tried to smile to let them know she was joking, but one wouldn't form. Maybe it wasn't as much of a joke as she'd first thought. Her parents treated her differently these days. It was nearly a minute before she could force herself to move. At the front door she turned to face Kellan. "I have no idea what I'm going to say to them."

"That you had fun?"

She reluctantly smiled. "I think they'd yell loud enough to wake the entire town if I said that." She looked from one to the other. "Thank you for walking me home."

"Anytime." Kellan raised his hands to the door in preparation for removing the wards so she could enter without setting them off.

"It was a pleasure," Rafe said.

"I'll meet both of you at Fable in the morning." Seeing Kellan lower his hands, she opened the door and slipped inside. She leaned against the door, listening to Kellan speaking softly, his words indistinguishable. Was it too late to run or had Kellan already set the wards?

Pushing away from the door, she silently made her way to the stairs and cautiously crept up them. She didn't want to wake her sister. It was bad enough her parents were awake. Her steps slowed as she approached her open bedroom door. They slowed further when her father spotted her and stopped pacing. She nearly froze when she saw the look in his eyes. Kellan's plan was looking worse by the second.

"Your grandfather was here about half an hour ago," Heron said.

She didn't need to ask which one. Maksim hadn't returned. "What did Grandfather Harlen want?" And what was he doing visiting so late?

"He heard about the prank you were involved in this evening. Are you trying to ruin our family?" Breena demanded. "What do you think the Duke will end up doing?"

She started to protest, closing her mouth when she realised she couldn't tell her parents that the Duke had been more amused than annoyed. That would lead to questions she couldn't answer.

"You've upset both the Duke and Duchess," Heron said. "What are your plans for tomorrow? To travel to the capital so you can upset the King?"

"We have to carry the Duke's flag through the streets tomorrow."

Heron momentarily closed his eyes. "We're ruined."

She had no reassurances for him. Feared what

would happen herself and dreaded having to tell both of them she was leaving town. Why had she insisted on going? Danton was right. She'd had no training. She was going to get herself killed.

"Have you anything to say for yourself?" Breena demanded.

"Sorry?"

"That's it?" Heron demanded. "You hold our family up to ridicule and all you can say is sorry. And you can't say it with conviction."

She barely managed to stop herself from saying sorry again.

"Well?" Heron took a step towards her.

Anger flared and she lowered her gaze, worried lightning might be visible in her eyes. They should be glad she was finding ways to make the town forget she was a necromancer. "I'm tired. I need to rise early in the morning. The Duke expects me at the castle at eight." She kept her gaze on the floor, staring at the timber boards.

Silence filled the room for several seconds, Heron breaking it. "You will stop spending time with Kellan and the vampire. Understand?"

She couldn't do that. "His name is Rafe."

"I don't care what his name is. You will stay away from him."

Meikah glanced towards her sister's door. She doubted her father would appreciate her telling him to keep his voice down so he didn't wake Ena.

"Understand?" Heron demanded.

"It's a little hard to stay away from them when the Duke expects us to parade through the streets together." She hesitated. "Can I go to sleep now?"

Heron strode from the room without a word, his steps heavy.

Breena remained where she was. "Do you want to end up back where my parents started? You'd never survive on the streets. We barely did."

She finally raised her head and met her mother's gaze. "There's no possibility I'd ever end up on the streets."

Breena stepped back with a sharp, indrawn breath. "Your eyes."

Meikah didn't need to look in a mirror to know Breena was talking about the lightning. She could feel the power coursing through her body. "I'm more likely to end up in the mountains than on the streets."

Breena started to reach for her, taking another step backwards instead. "I didn't want this for you."

She was tempted to apologise again, but she would have meant it as much as before. She tried to push away the anger she felt after seeing the flicker of fear in her mother's eyes. Fear of her rather than the usual fear for her. "I need to sleep."

Breena stared at her a moment longer before she walked away, not saying another word.

Chapter Six

Meikah turned and watched her mother stride towards her bedroom. Breena closed the door after one more glance at Meikah, fear remaining in her eyes. Meikah tried to convince herself she couldn't have seen clearly. A single lantern hung above the stairs, one of the few bewitched flames in the house. There'd been more than enough light. A sound had her spinning to face the door to her sister's room.

Ena remained in the doorway. "What did you do now?"

Answering wouldn't change her sister's accusatory tone so she didn't bother. Stepping into her room, she closed the door, leaning against it to stare at the candle on her chest of drawers, the flame reflected in the mirror that hung on the wall above the chest. She crossed the room to stare into her brown eyes, the flicker of lightning remaining in their depths. She didn't want this for herself either. Her hand rested on the hilt of her sword. She'd always expected to be a templar. The lightning flared. They weren't going to drive her out of town and she wasn't about to stay in the Dark Blade Academy where she not only didn't belong, but wasn't wanted.

Stripping down to her undergarments, she left her clothes and weapons on the chest of drawers, blowing out the candle before climbing into bed. Movement by the window had her sitting up again. "Kellan?"

"Yeah. Rafe too."

She felt one of them sit on the bed beside her. "I thought you were going back to Fable."

Rafe took her hand. "We wanted to see that you were all right first."

She should have known it was Rafe sitting on her bed with how well he could see in the dark. "I'm fine. Both of you go home." She drew her hand from his.

Rafe leaned close. "We never would have met if you couldn't see the dead."

He moved away before she could say anything.

"Goodnight." Kellan's voice came from beside the window.

She stared at the area, seeing the movement of his shadow. "Goodnight." They blocked the light that came in the window. Then they were gone, moonlight filtering through to cast a soft light on the window ledge. Remaining sitting, she stared at the curtain that swayed in the breeze, reducing and increasing the light with its movement. Dread for the next morning pooled in her. Would she have to face the Duchess too?

Her mouth dropped open and power rushed through her. Somehow she'd successfully done her first prank. Her lips curved into a smile. A complicated, crazy prank that she'd been certain would fail. The rumours would fly around the town. And they wouldn't be about her being a necromancer. Lying down, she pushed the power away, struggling to make it obey. Smiling, she tried to imagine what Kellan would look like in a chemise. Was it large enough to fit him? A giggle escaped at the thought of his broad shoulders filling out the garment and the seams possibly breaking apart. She'd find out soon enough.

The power eventually seeped away and she drifted off to sleep, her dreams filled with lightning, fire and mist. A banging on her door woke her in the morning and she glared at it, too tired to move. From the amount of light in her room, the sun must have barely risen. "What?"

"You've got a visitor."

Ena's tone had Meikah sitting up, staring at the door. She didn't sound happy. "Who?" She stumbled out of bed, pulling on her clothes and buckling on weapons.

"He wouldn't say. He also wouldn't come inside."

Dressed, Meikah opened the door. "I can't see who it is if you don't get out of the way." It was early enough the bewitched flame burned in the hallway lantern.

"I heard what you did. Grandfather Harlen just left. It's a wonder the yelling didn't wake you."

She'd been tired enough to sleep through anything. Even a horde of zombies. "Out of the way."

"Don't you care?"

"Which rumours do you prefer?"

"What?" Ena frowned.

"Do you want people talking about me being a necromancer or that I'm getting into trouble with Kellan?" She nearly grinned when Ena's mouth remained open. Pushing past her sister, she headed for the stairs.

Ena hurried after her. "Is he one too?"

"He seemed like the person to approach when I needed to create rumours." She let the grin escape. "After all, he's really good at it."

"They would have forgotten. If you'd done nothing, the rumours would have died down."

She paused at the bottom of the stairs, Ena several steps above her. "No, they wouldn't. It's not the sort of thing people forget." She strode to the front door, opening it.

"Are you ready?" Shade's hood of his jacket was up, hiding his face from view.

"I haven't eaten." Nor had she expected anyone to come for her this early. Or even turn up to collect her.

"We'll feed you." He stepped away from the doorway.

"I-" She broke off when her sister came to stand behind her. "All right." She looked over her shoulder. "Tell our parents I've left already."

Ena grabbed her arm, preventing her from leaving, letting go when a dagger appeared in Shade's hand. "They want to speak to you."

She couldn't handle a lecture first thing in the morning. "I'll talk to them later." When she had to tell them the news that the Duchess was sending her on a task as punishment for swimming in her fountain.

"But-" Ena started to reach for her, drawing back her hand after a glance at Shade.

"I'll see you later." Meikah walked away, glancing towards the house as she stepped onto the footpath,

Shade at her side. Ena remained in the doorway, watching her. She felt a moment of sympathy for her sister. Telling their parents that she'd left wouldn't be pleasant. "You didn't have to take out a dagger."

Shade shrugged. "Family can be as dangerous as strangers."

"We're templars, not dark blades."

"You aren't. Not anymore."

She couldn't argue with that comment, even though she'd automatically started to. It was going to take time before she could think of herself as something else. Something she couldn't tell anyone she was. "What does everyone think you do?"

"Who?"

"Your family."

"That I'm one of the guards for Fable." He shrugged. "I don't tell them much."

"Why would people think a bookshop needs guards?"

"Some of the books are priceless. We've had our share of sorcerers trying to take rather than purchase. Necros too."

She started to ask him what had happened when another question occurred to her. "Why were you sent to get me?"

"Kellan is busy arguing with Flint. He wants to leave now. Kellan thinks you should travel together."

"He's going without us?" The roads weren't safe. Flint hadn't wanted to take them with him in the first place. Didn't think they were capable of helping. Was this his way of trying to get rid of them?

"Danton won't let me go with you even though Flint's planning on going ahead."

Now it made sense. "Are the others expecting me?"

Shade glanced at her. "No."

"We'll look out for each other. Livia will be fine." Thoughts of what the roads were like crept in. Bandits were the least of their problems.

"Help them talk Flint into waiting." Shade stopped outside the front door of Fable and faced her.

She nodded. "I'll see what I can do." She guessed Shade must have thought one extra to argue for waiting would help.

Shade opened the door, holding it while she entered, following her in.

Mace stood behind the counter grinning, jerking his head towards the curtained doorway where the argument could be heard. "Come to join the fun?"

"Why aren't you in there if you think it's so much fun?" Meikah walked towards the counter.

"I was chased out. Flint said my opinion didn't count since I wasn't going."

Meikah glanced towards Shade, who nodded. And there was the real reason Shade had collected her. "All right. I'll talk to Flint." She doubted he'd listen to her since no one else seemed to lately. Not her parents and certainly not Harlen. She stepped around the counter and through the curtained doorway, the hallway shadowy and dim after being outside.

Rafe appeared, grabbing hold of her hand as she passed the stairs leading up, drawing her to him. "Amiel won't take a message for me."

"Is it safe to come out of the basement?" She glanced at the open trapdoor under the stairs.

"Sunlight doesn't come this far into the building. Ask Kellan if he can have the Duke send us off the moment we finish the parade through the streets. We can keep going and meet up with Flint on the outskirts of town. Livia, Shade and Mace can pack what we might need and Livia can wait with Flint for us."

She grinned. That'd get her out of having to return home. "I'll see what Kellan says." When Rafe let go of her hand, she continued to the kitchen, stopping in the doorway. "Rafe has a suggestion."

Kellan stopped mid-word and faced her. "Why are you here so early?"

He should have been the one to send for her, not Shade. "Did you want to hear Rafe's suggestion?"

"This is a waste of time." Flint continued to wear his mask.

"I want to hear his suggestion." Livia sent a glare to Flint before she returned her gaze to Meikah.

"Go ahead," Danton said.

Chapter Seven

Meikah repeated Rafe's suggestion and waited for Kellan's answer. When he slowly nodded, she began to think it was a possibility.

"I'll give you until nine," Flint said. "You take longer than that and I leave."

"That's only an hour. We'll need longer than that," Livia protested.

Flint shrugged. "You're Assassins Of The Dead. You should be ready to go at a moment's notice."

"They would be ready if it wasn't for needing a cover story." Danton stood near the table, his arms crossed over his broad chest.

Kellan turned to Livia. "Grab me parchment and writing implements."

"Get it yourself."

"Livia." Danton's tone was mild, but it was enough

to get the shapeshifter moving, muttering under her breath as she left the kitchen, brushing past Meikah.

"Two hours," Kellan said to Flint.

Flint shook his head. "Suri has been on her own at Longview for nearly a month."

"Who is Suri?" Meikah stepped out of the way as Livia strode back towards the table.

Livia slammed the inkpot and quill on the table, tossing parchment beside them. "She's Flint's partner." She faced Flint. "We're not asking you to wait all day."

Kellan sat at the table. "Waiting is beneficial for you too. The roads are dangerous. Once we reach the mountains the creatures are a bigger worry than bandits. And the dragons are a greater problem when we get further into the mountains." He uncorked the bottle of ink and dipped the quill in it.

"Nine. Not a minute later," Flint said.

Kellan looked up at him for a second then nodded. "I'll tell the Duke we're turning up at half past seven for our lecture from the Duchess." He dipped the quill into the ink again.

"If he doesn't agree, that's your problem." Flint strode out the back door and into the alley.

Kellan shook the parchment a few times before he folded it. "I'll see if Mace or Shade will deliver this while I pack for the journey and finish getting ready for the parade. We don't have a lot of time left to get ready if we're going to be at the castle by half past seven."

"I'll deliver it." Shade stepped out of the doorway leading to the hallway.

Kellan handed the parchment to Shade, glancing over his shoulder to Meikah. "Coming?"

She hurried after him, checking under the stairs for Rafe. He was gone. Upstairs, she followed Kellan to the room the spare outfits were stored in, along with numerous weapons. "What are we doing?"

"We'll live in our outfits and masks while we're in Longview. It's what we do when we're away on a mission." Kellan opened one of the wardrobes and began to take out garments in three different colours. Grey, charcoal and navy.

"How are we meant to eat with a full face mask on?"

"We have half face masks we use when we leave Dreyton."

Meikah stared at the pile of clothes Kellan held. "I want something better than these. Something like what Flint has. I'd hate to be stuck in these if I died."

"Necros can't die," Kellan said absently. He

grabbed a sturdy, cloth backpack, shoving the outfits in it.

"But their bodies can be killed and I don't want to be stuck in these ugly clothes if that happens. Why does Flint have a better outfit?"

"It's battle gear and it's expensive. Livia and Mace have some. They're the only ones who've finished growing."

She didn't want to wait that long. "Where do you buy them?"

Kellan slung the backpack onto his shoulder. "You don't. We send measurements to the Assassins Of The Dead faction in the capital and they have someone who makes the outfit and sends it to us."

"So I can't get one?" She followed him out of the room to the last door along the hallway on the left, stopping in the doorway when she realised it was his room. "I need things from home to take with me."

Kellan dropped the backpack onto the bed. "You can't pack yet. How would you explain that to your family? We'll send Shade for your gear. He's the quietest one."

"I'm not having him rifling in my underwear drawer."

"Write out a list and he can give it to whoever is home and explain the official excuse."

"All right." She took a step backwards when he began to unbutton his shirt. "I'll do that now." She fled downstairs, the sound of Kellan's laughter following her.

Rafe drew her under the stairs before she could leave the hallway. "Are you fine? You sounded… distressed."

She pulled away from his grip. "It's rude to listen in on conversations." She started to move away.

Rafe drew her back. "What is going on between you and Kellan?"

She sighed heavily. "Nothing." She paused a moment. "How can I ever choose one of you over the other? Wouldn't that be awkward since we work together?"

"Are you trying to find a polite way to turn me down?"

She shook her head. "I don't-" She pulled away from him, shaking her head again. "This is too-" She broke off when every word she thought of wasn't quite right. Confusing? Difficult? Strange? She had no idea. "I have to make a list." This time he didn't stop her from entering the kitchen. She stopped when she saw Amiel pacing the floor. "Where were you earlier?"

"Staying out of sight of the assassin."

"Why?"

"I don't need people knowing my business," Amiel said.

Mace entered the kitchen, stepping around Meikah. "In other words he's probably worried his past will catch up with him." He took a pan down and set it on top of the woodstove, glancing over his shoulder. "You hungry?"

"I was promised breakfast." She sat at the table, drawing parchment towards herself and reaching for the quill, ignoring Amiel's muttering.

"Oat cakes?"

She nodded as she began her list, trying to think of what she'd need. "How long do you think we'll be gone?"

Mace put the ingredients he'd taken out of the pantry onto the table along with a mixing bowl. "It'll probably take around fifteen hours to reach Longview. Longer if you run into trouble."

So there was around two days in travel. "And how long will it take to deal with an army of zombies?"

"You could be gone for days or it might be months." Mace threw ingredients into the bowl.

"Pack light," Amiel said. "Don't they teach you anything these days?"

"They won't be travelling all that light. They'll

need to take a wagon with them." Mace dropped batter into the pan, the mix sizzling.

She crossed out a couple of items on her list and added several others. By the time she'd finished the food was ready and everyone joined her at the table, Kellan wearing a hooded robe. Shade had arrived when the food was ready and she gave the list to him when he agreed to take it to her family later.

Mace sat down, helping himself from the pile of flat oat cakes in the middle of the table. "Ask Rafe if he wants us to bring him any." Mace glanced at Amiel.

"I'm not a messenger."

Meikah began to rise from the table. "I'll go."

Mace put out a hand to stop her from rising completely. "Amiel can go. He's not doing anything." Mace stared at Amiel until he strode from the room.

Chapter Eight

Meikah looked between Mace and the direction Amiel had taken. "What's going on?"

"He left me to guard the place while he hid. Told me I wasn't doing anything. Only sleeping."

Livia laughed. "No wonder you were cranky when I asked why you were awake so early."

Danton held a leather moneybag out to Kellan. "Send regular updates of what is happening if you need to stay a while. Let me know if things are more than you can handle and I'll contact the capital."

A muffled jingle of coins sounded as Kellan took the bag and slid it under his robe. "We know the drill."

"Make sure you don't get caught." Danton reached for another oat cake.

There was laughter around the table. A smile remained on Meikah's lips when she met Livia's gaze and saw the humour in her eyes that were a shade lighter than her auburn coloured hair.

Amiel entered the kitchen. "Said he was fine. Doesn't need food, only blood. But thanked you for thinking of him as food is an enjoyable pastime."

Danton rose from the table. "You had best leave for the castle." He looked to Mace. "Bring the wagon around to the back and we'll meet you out there with the coffin."

It didn't take long to chain the coffin closed, once Rafe was inside, and take it upstairs and out the back to where Mace drew up with a flat bed wagon. Shade hefted a chest onto the wagon behind the timber slat seat, tying it in place. "I'll wait with Livia and Flint after I've collected Meikah's gear." He drew up the hood of his jacket. "I'll give the Duchess time to tell you about your punishment first."

Mace patted the seat beside him. "Want to join me, Meikah? Kellan can sit with Rafe."

She clambered up beside Mace, waving to Amiel who stood in the doorway. She grinned when he turned away without returning her wave. Her gaze was drawn to Livia and Shade, standing arm in arm. "I'll see you soon."

Mace urged the horses forward. "A pity we can't all go."

Kellan was sitting on the coffin behind them. "Shade is going to be impossible to live with. Livia is one of us. He should know we're not about to let anything happen to her."

Meikah turned on her seat to face Kellan. "Should you be sitting there?"

Kellan laughed, knocking on the timber. "You mind if I use your coffin as a seat?"

"Do I have a choice?" Rafe's voice was muffled.

Kellan laughed again. "Probably not. You take up a lot of space."

Meikah tried to see under the hood of the robe when she caught a glimpse of reflected light. "What are you wearing?"

"You'll find out soon enough."

"Sure to be something that'll keep the gossips going," Mace said.

"Of course," Kellan said.

Meikah faced forward as they came closer to the castle. "Does anyone other than the Duke know who you really are?"

"He'll know who you are soon enough, if he doesn't already know by now," Mace said.

"Should I be worried about him finding out?" She looked from Mace to Kellan. It was annoying that she couldn't see Kellan's expression.

"Only if he wants something from you." Mace grinned, pulling up the hood on his jacket, casting his face into shadows.

"What would he want?"

"Your service to the town." Kellan said. "Which can be more dangerous than facing an army of zombies."

She fell silent as they drove through the castle gates, the guards watching them. A glance around the area showed there were more than guards watching their passing. People were scattered around the courtyard, most of them not bothering to pretend they were doing anything other than gawking.

Mace pulled up near the castle entrance. "We'll wait here for you."

Meikah tried to swallow. It had become an effort. She hopped off the wagon to stand beside Kellan. "Remind me never to agree to another one of your pranks."

"Not likely." He swept off his robe and held out an arm to her.

Meikah stared at him. The chemise looked like it might break apart at the seams, the thins straps tight across his muscular shoulders. But it wasn't that which drew her attention. He'd dressed his hair, jewelled clips holding it in place, and painted his face to look like a lady about to attend a ball at the castle. Yet there was no mistaking he was male. "The Duke will banish us permanently."

Mace twisted in the seat to knock on the coffin. "You're missing a sight being stuck in there."

Kellan took her hand and placed it on his forearm. "Hold your head up and act like you're attending a ball."

"I feel underdressed."

Kellan laughed, the rich sound ringing out in the courtyard as they walked up the stairs, the guards letting them into the castle, shocked expressions on their faces. "I wouldn't let it bother you. I'll take you to the next ball and you can dress up then."

"I've never been to a ball. I have no idea what people wear to one." Her grip tightened on his arm. "Why did I say I'd share your punishment?"

Kellan stopped and faced her, taking her hand that was resting on his arm and raising it to his lips, his gaze holding hers. He placed her hand on his shoulder, moving closer to rest a hand on her waist and taking hold of her other hand. "May I have this dance?" He spun her around, dancing her towards the reception room.

The faces of those watching became a blur and she tried to focus on not tripping over, her gaze on

Kellan's face. "You are crazy." Her voice was soft, not wanting her words to carry to those who watched them.

Kellan grinned. "Of course." He whirled them around one more time, letting go of her waist to raise her hand and bow to the Duke and Duchess. "Your Graces. We are here as requested."

The Duke looked Kellan up and down. "Not exactly as requested." His gaze rested on Kellan's black hair. "I see you couldn't resist adding your own touches."

"Why thank you for noticing, Your Grace." Kellan bowed again.

The Duke waved Meikah forward, waiting until she was closer before he spoke softly. "Rumours will always follow you if you continue to follow him."

"There are worse rumours, Your Grace." She kept her gaze on the floor, glancing up in time to see the Duke look at Kellan, who nodded.

The Duke's gaze returned to Meikah. "Yes, there are. I'm sorry to hear that." He glanced at a footman, gesturing him over. The lad carried the Duke's flag on a pole. "Your flag bearer. He'll go ahead of you. We have decided it's best we send another to carry the flag for you."

Meikah stepped back next to Kellan guessing, or rather hoping, the Duke had finished talking to her.

The Duchess nodded at her husband's words, her light brown hair dressed more elaborately than Kellan's, a glint of humour in her blue eyes. "Who knows what mess you'd make of the task if we left it up to you."

"Thoughtful as ever, Your Grace." Kellan stepped forward to take the Duchess' hand and raise it to his lips.

She drew her hand back before he could kiss it. "Do not think to charm me young man. You will not get off lightly for swimming in my fountain."

Kellan bowed. "I will accept whatever Your Grace says I deserve."

Meikah tried not to look at the many faces that surrounded them. It felt like a nightmare with the sea of people filling the room. She nearly fled when she spotted her grandfather. Harlen's expression was thunderous. Looking away from him, she tried to focus on what the Duchess was saying, wondering what she might have missed.

"Everyone knows there are no finer silk scarves than those to be found at King's Peak."

Kellan nodded at the Duchess' words. "As always, you are right, Your Grace."

"You and your companions will fetch one for me."

A murmur filled the reception room, growing louder as the gossiping began.

"Personally, Your Grace?"

Meikah was impressed with the confused expression Kellan managed.

The Duchess inclined her head. "It might keep you out of mischief for a time. The flag bearer will lead you through the town and leave you on the outskirts. You may return to Dreyton after you have personally obtained a silk scarf from King's Peak for me."

Kellan bowed over the Duchess' hand. This time she allowed him to raise it to his lips. "I am ever at your command, Your Grace."

"Then maybe in future you can refrain from swimming in my fountain."

"Of course, Your Grace. It was a slight misjudgement on my part."

"You tend to have many such misjudgements from what I have noticed."

Meikah stared at the Duchess. Was she trying not to smile?

The Duchess waved her hand regally. "You may leave."

Chapter Nine

Meikah bowed when Kellan did so. Although she supposed Kellan should have curtseyed since that was what was expected when wearing a dress. She was grateful he took hold of her hand as they walked through the crowd. It seemed to have grown in size since they'd entered. She tried to avoid Harlen's gaze. When she saw him push through the crowd towards her, she wanted to sprint for the wagon. Kellan's grip on her hand tightened and she kept the same pace he maintained.

The swell of sound behind them continued to rise and if it hadn't been for Kellan, she would have run. Not only from the room, but also from the town. So much for not allowing them to chase her from her home. How could he remain calm? Everyone was talking about him too. Stepping outside, she was relieved to see Mace continued to wait.

Mace looked past them. "Didn't they trust you with the flag?"

Meikah checked over her shoulder, having forgotten about the boy who was to carry the flag. She forgot about him again when she saw Harlen stride towards her, leaving the crowd behind. It was too late to run. Probably had been the moment she'd let Kellan help her start rumours.

Harlen stopped in front of her, keeping his voice low. "What do I tell your parents?"

"That I'm off to see some of the country?" The words escaped before she could prevent them.

"I warned you not to shame our family." His lips barely moved, his voice threateningly low.

Kellan stepped closer. "You might want to rethink those words. You're the one about to cause a scene."

She tugged Kellan back, meeting Harlen's angry gaze. "Maybe you should talk to my parents and find out exactly what's going on." She lowered her voice further. "Have there been any rumours of necromancy lately?" Turning away, she strode after the boy carrying the flag, Kellan at her side. Behind she heard the wheels of the wagon on the cobblestones.

"Are you all right?" Kellan waved to those they passed, smiling and nodding in greeting.

She had no idea. If anything, she was feeling a little stunned by everything. "I don't think the Duke is expecting you to behave like visiting royalty during the parade. It's meant to be a punishment."

Kellan blew a kiss to a group of ladies watching them, turning to wave at a cluster on the other side of the road. "Is it? Or is it another opportunity to keep the gossips talking?" He met her gaze. "Try it." He grinned. "Dare you."

She couldn't resist returning his grin. "You're crazy."

He captured her hand, raising it to his lips. "Of course." Raising both his hands above his head, continuing to hold onto hers, he raised his voice. "You're all too kind turning out to see me like this. Thank you. Thank you." He nodded in both directions.

Meikah waved to a group on her left, surprised when some of them waved back. She looked in the other direction as Kellan lowered his hands, keeping hold of hers. She waved in that direction too. Her grin widened when a young man bowed, two young ladies waved and a child jumped up and down waving both hands. Laughter bubbled up. No wonder Kellan kept telling her pranks were fun. How did he end up with a punishment like this when she got threatened with groundings whenever she did something wrong?

They followed the flag bearer to the outskirts of town, laughter trailing them along with people who seemed to know Kellan well enough to ask him how he felt about the upcoming journey. One young lady asked him to bring her back a scarf too.

Kellan laughed. "How could I do that? The Duchess would banish me if I brought back a scarf for another."

Meikah worried the crowd would follow them all the way out of town. The closer they came to the outskirts, the more people drifted away until there was only a handful left by the time they reached the meeting place. Those drifted away when Kellan thanked the flag bearer, waving goodbye to the last of the crowd.

Livia slipped out of Shade's arms, taking Mace's place on the wagon. Flint remained at a distance and Kellan pulled his robe on, drawing up the hood once he'd removed the jewelled clips, his black hair falling down his back.

Shade gave Meikah a cloth bag. "Your sister said to thank you."

Meikah stared speechlessly at him for a moment. "Are you sure it was my sister?"

Shade nodded. "It was the one at the door with you this morning. She looks a lot like you. Has the same dark eyes, although her hair is short. Also more arrogant than you."

"I'm not arrogant." Raising her chin, she glared at him.

Shade laughed softly. "There it is. The same arrogant look your sister gave me."

Livia laughed. "What did you expect, Shade?"

Shade turned away from Meikah to leap onto the wagon beside Livia, drawing her up from where she sat on the seat. "Don't get caught."

Meikah looked away from their kiss, noticing Flint had begun to ride away. A bow and quiver hung at his back. "Time to leave."

Kellan looked in the same direction. "He could have waited for us to say goodbye." He clapped Mace on the shoulder. "Look out for Danton." He dropped the jewelled clips into Mace's hand. "And see that my sister gets these. You might want to leave them in her room rather than give them to her." He hopped back onto the wagon, knocking on the coffin as he sat on top of it. "We're about to leave town."

"I do sleep days." Rafe's muffled voice held a note of irritation.

Meikah joined Livia on the seat, barely space for three.

Shade kissed Livia one more time before he leapt to the ground, slipping into the shadows of a building as he watched them leave.

Meikah turned to watch the town fall behind. "I've never left Dreyton before."

Kellan clasped her hand tightly. "We'll be back before you have time to miss the place."

She didn't bother telling him she already missed it. Drawing her hand from his, she faced forward. Flint remained ahead of them, the distance increasing once they left town and Kellan asked Livia to pull up so he could slip into the forest, which pressed up close to each side of the dirt road, to change his clothes. He returned, wearing dark trousers and a shirt like Livia and Meikah wore, his hair once again tied at the nape of his neck. He wiped at his face with the chemise, cleaning off the powders.

"Did you have fun on the parade?" Kellan leapt onto the wagon, putting the robe and chemise in the large trunk he'd taken his gear from, taking out Meikah's night blades and holding them out to her.

Surprised, she took them from him, giving him her other weapons to put in the chest. "It wasn't what I expected." She strapped on the blades, not sure she should tell him she'd actually enjoyed herself. Knowing Kellan he'd take that as permission to plan something else equally crazy.

"Flint better not be planning to ride through the night. I'll want a break eventually." Livia urged the horses forward. "He could have waited a few more minutes for us."

Flint continued riding until the sun set, unable to see the path in the dark. Rafe offered to drive the wagon and Flint tied his horse to the back once they'd taken a short break. Meikah remained on the seat with Rafe while Livia laughingly took over his coffin, leaving the lid off at Rafe's warning that it was airtight.

The wagon started forward as Livia spoke. "This is surprisingly comfortable. I'm exhausted enough I could fall asleep in here."

"Be careful you don't make it permanent," Flint muttered.

"We can't die," Livia said.

"Our bodies can," Flint reminded her.

Chapter Ten

Meikah tried to think of something to say to change the subject, preferring not to talk about dying. She gave up when everyone remained silent. At some stage, she drifted off to sleep, waking when Rafe nudged her, shushing her when she would have spoken.

"Wake everyone." His voice was little more than a breath of air.

She leaned close to speak to him. "I can't see."

"Feel your way."

"What's wrong?"

"I don't know, but the place is filled with the scents of other creatures, the smell of death and the horses are unsettled."

Feeling her way into the back of the wagon, she found Livia first. The shapeshifter was asleep in the coffin. Meikah covered her mouth with her hand, bending close. "Shh. Rafe smells something."

Livia pushed her hand away, breathing in deeply. "A lot of somethings by the smell of it."

Flint moved closer to them, his bow in his hand, shuffling alongside the coffin. "You sense them watching you?" He spoke softly.

"Smell them," Livia said.

Meikah patted the bed of the wagon, looking for Kellan. She found his shoulder first, clamping her hand over his mouth when he started to speak. She drew her hand away when he kissed it.

Kellan reached for her, his hand holding hers as he moved closer. "What's going on?"

"Something is out there." She heard Kellan move towards Rafe and followed, wincing when she ran into the trunk behind the seat. She reached them partway through the conversation.

"I don't know," Rafe said.

"I'll get the lanterns and hang them on the wagon ready to be lit. Call out light the moment whatever is out there starts to move in on us," Kellan said.

Once Kellan had moved past her, she rejoined Rafe on the seat, her hand resting on the hilt of her sword, glad she wore the dagger that matched the night blade at her other side. She tried to see into the darkness. It was impossible. Looking up didn't help either. Starlight and moonlight couldn't penetrate the tree canopy. A sound drew her attention. She stared into the darkness, unable to see anything. "What was that noise?"

"I don't know. Whatever it was is staying out of sight."

A clattering sound came from the wagon and Flint cursed softly.

Meikah looked over her shoulder even though she already knew she wouldn't be able to see anything. She turned to Rafe. "What's it like to be able to see in the dark?" She stared towards him, waiting for an answer. "Rafe?"

"Light!" Rafe drew the horses to a stop, leaping from the wagon, daggers in his hands, flames sliding along the blades.

Four lanterns flared to light.

Flint hissed at the sight of the warriors coming towards them. "It's the newly dead." He drew back an arrow.

"Sentient zombies." Kellan leapt to the ground, sword in hand. He glanced at Livia. "At least these ones shouldn't taste as bad as rotting zombies."

Meikah drew both her sword and dagger, jumping

down to stand between Kellan and Rafe, waiting for the zombies to reach them.

Livia stood on the back of the wagon. "They still smell of the grave. That sickly sweet scent. I don't care if they're sentient. If they come after me, I'm tearing their throats out." She looked past them. "And the throats of whatever else is hiding in the forest."

"What are they waiting for?" Meikah asked.

"Assessing the situation. There'll be a leader who's deciding what to do," Kellan said.

The bewitched flames clearly showed eleven sentient zombies, various weapons held ready. How was she meant to kill what were basically living, breathing people? Most of them were dressed in the clothes they'd probably died in. Only one of them wore armour.

"Him." Rafe pointed to the armoured zombie. "We take him out and the rest will have no leader."

"We have to get to him first. They keep moving around him making it impossible to fire at him," Flint said.

"I'm not about to stand around here all night waiting for them to make the first move. For all we know they've called for reinforcements." Livia leapt forward, turning into a sleek, black mountain cat in mid jump. She snarled, going for the closest zombie.

Rafe followed, attacking a zombie that went for Livia, his blades slicing through the air.

"This will not end well," Flint muttered, releasing an arrow.

Kellan cursed.

Meikah turned to see more zombies coming out of the forest.

"I hate it when Livia's right. She never predicts anything cheerful." Kellan ran towards the half a dozen zombies that came at him, others running out of the forest to join those attacking.

Meikah tightened her grip on her weapons, power rising and lightning rushing along the blades. She ran towards the zombies Kellan attacked, fighting off another one who tried to get at him. She'd barely beheaded the zombie she fought when he was replaced by two others.

Rafe joined her before the zombies could surround her, laying about with his flaming daggers.

Meikah didn't have the chance to thank him. She was kept busy fighting. More zombies came towards her. They should have brought Mace and Shade. How were they meant to survive a zombie army?

Livia leapt in front of Meikah, tearing into one of the zombies before launching herself at another one. The zombies kept coming.

A woman wearing a half mask came out of the forest, dressed in Assassins Of The Dead battle gear. She wielded a battleaxe, the blade crackling with lightning as it sank into the zombies. "About time you arrived, Flint."

Flint stood on the back of the wagon, firing his arrows into zombies, Kellan attacking those that came close. "I had trouble finding help. Why aren't you at Longview?"

Meikah guessed the woman was Suri. They were going to need more than one extra assassin to survive the battle. She kept her sword in motion, her dagger blocking an attack before she was forced to jump out of the way of another zombie.

"Saw this lot heading out and tracked them. Didn't expect you to be wandering the forest in the dark." Suri cleaved a zombie in two. "Although you've got enough lanterns for it to be nearly daylight."

"You up to a storm?" Flint shot a zombie as it tried to clamber up on the wagon, Kellan busy with several zombies on the other side. "Before the numbers overwhelm us."

Suri nodded. "Bring the rain." She kept swinging about her with her battleaxe.

Meikah saw clouds form above them, the area over

the wagon clear. Rain wasn't about to make fighting any easier. Especially if the ground turned to mud.

"In the wagon," Flint ordered.

They all obeyed, Livia tearing out the throat of one more zombie before she joined them. Flint fired an arrow at a zombie that tried to follow, Kellan slashing at one coming up on the other side.

Meikah started to ask why they'd retreated. Her question was interrupted before she could make a sound.

"Now," Flint called out.

Suri flung out a hand, lightning crackling around it, arrowing towards the rain that fell, connecting and combining, striking the advancing zombies. A crack of thunder sounded as the lightning burst through the area, tearing zombies apart. The rain and lightning ended abruptly and Suri staggered.

Meikah stared at them open mouthed. No wonder people feared necromancers.

Flint was at Suri's side in seconds, an arm around her waist. "What are you lot waiting for? Finish off the stragglers."

Livia snarled before she leapt from the wagon, seizing hold of a zombie that ran towards them. Rafe followed Livia, Kellan heading in the other direction.

Chapter Eleven

Closing her mouth, Meikah looked in both directions before following Kellan, stepping over the fallen bodies. It didn't take them long to deal with the handful of zombies that were left and she returned to the wagon, Kellan at her side.

A bow remained in Flint's hand and he scanned the area, Suri leaning against the trunk, her eyes closed.

Livia leapt onto the back of the wagon before she turned human. "She going to be all right?" Livia nodded towards Suri.

"It takes a lot of energy to wield so much power," Flint said.

Suri opened her eyes, smiling slightly. "I'll be good as new come morning." She closed her eyes again.

"How did you do that?" Meikah looked from Suri's hands to her own. Why did they need help if they were able to take out a horde of zombies on their own? How many zombies had descended on Longview that Flint and Suri needed help?

"Practice," Flint said.

Suri laughed softly, her eyes opening again. "Nearly getting ourselves killed too many times to count while we were trying to perfect the move."

"That too." Flint turned to Rafe. "Ready to drive the rest of the way? It's not much further to Longview."

Kellan opened the trunk once Suri sat forward. "We'll get dressed in our gear." He handed outfits to each of them before heading into the forest to change.

Meikah found a large tree to stand behind, the lanterns hanging on the wagon giving her enough light to be able to see. She changed into the navy coloured outfit Kellan had given her, relieved to see she only had a half mask to wear. Returning to the wagon she found she was the last one to arrive. She put her other clothes in the corner of the chest with the ones her companions had already placed inside.

Livia extinguished the lights before Rafe urged the horses forward.

"Can't we keep one of the lanterns on?" Meikah tried to see into the night. "I can't see anything."

"It wouldn't help," Livia said. "You wouldn't be able to see past the shadows of the trees. I barely can."

Suri, who sat on top of the trunk, leaning against Flint, spoke. "There's nothing to see."

"You can see in the dark?" Meikah asked.

"My father is a shapeshifter, my mother human. All I inherited from him was his ability to see in the dark."

Meikah didn't feel any better to know they had three who could see approaching zombies. She wanted to know what might be coming for them.

"Some necros learn to see in the dark," Kellan said.

"How?" That was a skill that could come in handy. She almost asked Kellan if he could see in the dark, but then decided he would have said he could if he was able to or if he wanted Flint and Suri to know.

"Sorcerers can do it. Or at least ones who learn the ability," Livia said.

"Not many learn how to see in the dark," Flint said. "There are usually more important things to learn first."

"Vampires can see in the dark," Rafe said.

"You don't want to become a vampire," Suri said.

"Why not?" Rafe demanded.

"Because your strengths don't outweigh your weaknesses. The zombies are slaughtering the vampires of Longview. Day arrives and they attack. There are a dozen humans left to protect the place during the day and not many more vampires to guard the town of a night," Suri said.

"I tried to get back sooner," Flint said. "No one could help. Too many necromancers causing problems around the country."

"I knew you'd be back as soon as you could." Suri's quiet words were the last spoken until they reached Longview.

A voice called out from beside the wagon, startling Meikah. "About time you got back, Flint."

She looked in the direction the voice came from. "Can we have the lanterns on now?" The handful of lights visible in the town didn't reach them.

Two of the lanterns hanging on the wagon flared to life, Livia lowering a hand. "Better?"

Meikah returned Livia's grin. "Not much."

"Daylight is worse," Suri warned. "Night is the safest around here."

"The stable is over that way." The vampire who'd called out earlier pointed out the direction. He was grinning, canine teeth visible. "We were beginning to think something had happened to you. Good to see you again, Flint. Nice to see you brought help."

Rafe turned the horses towards the stable, pulling them up in front of a building that looked empty. "Where are the rest of the horses?"

"We sent most of the humans away. Those who weren't capable of fighting. They needed the horses to pull wagons and carriages." The vampire looked in the direction Meikah and her companions had come from. "There aren't many places willing to take in vampires."

Kellan stepped forward, holding out his hand. "I'm Kellan."

Meikah wanted to ask him why he gave his real name instead of using the nickname he used in Dreyton.

The vampire shook Kellan's hand. "Devin." He glanced towards the stable. "You might want to stay in the stable loft. It's one of the few buildings that's intact and easily defended."

A vampire strode towards them, her long blond hair braided back from her face. "Don't go telling them that. We don't want them to leave." She stopped in front of Kellan, holding out her hand. "Sarette. Welcome to my town. If there's anything you need, let me know." She was dressed in black, from her long sleeved shirt to her trousers and embroidered vest. Even her knee high boots were black.

"What about a building with a basement?" Rafe joined Sarette and Kellan.

Sarette tugged at his chin as she turned his face

from one side to the other. "I thought Flint was fetching more who can see spirits in case they change their tactics of only sending zombies. You're a vampire."

Rafe barred his teeth, showing his fangs. "I can see spirits and wield elemental magic."

"Which element?"

"Fire." Rafe grinned when Sarette took half a step back. "That seems to be the usual response."

Meikah tried not to yawn, but was unsuccessful. "It's been a long journey and-"

Sarette interrupted Meikah. "I apologise for not being a better host. I'll see that pallets are set up in the stable loft for you and food prepared." She looked towards Devin who moved away in a blur.

Meikah stared after him. It was odd to see someone else move with the same speed as Rafe. She returned her attention to Sarette. "Thank you."

It didn't take long for an area to be prepared and food to be brought to the loft where they waited. Rafe had offered to guard the building while they slept, having first taken his coffin to the loft with Kellan's help. Flint and Suri went to the cottage they were staying in.

Meikah picked at the food, too tired to want to eat even though she was hungry. "Is it possible to talk?"

Kellan shook his head.

"There are things I want to know." She'd expected to be able to have her questions answered once they were alone. She'd forgotten about the vampire ability of exceptional hearing.

Kellan moved close, his lips against her ear. "What did you want to know?"

She turned her head so she could whisper into his ear. "Why use your name instead of your nickname?"

"No one knows where we come from and would have no idea who we are."

That made sense. "Can you see in the dark?"

"Not as well as a shapeshifter or vampire. It's like those moments before dusk when there's very little light, but you can see most of what's happening."

"I want to learn."

Kellan chuckled before he leaned close again. "There are other things you need to learn first. It isn't easy."

"How did you learn?"

"At the Spell Sword Academy."

"Oh."

Livia moved closer. "What's going on?"

"Things you already know," Kellan said.

"Then I'm off to bed."

Meikah finished her food. "Bed sounds good."

Livia raised her hand. "Want me to put out the lantern?"

"Give me time to get into bed." Meikah left her weapons beside her pallet and kicked off her boots. "Aren't you taking off your masks?"

"Yeah." Kellan removed his mask and weapons before he lay down, leaving his boots on.

"Should I have left my boots on?" Meikah looked from Kellan to Livia noticing both had left theirs on.

"I'm tired enough I'd probably be able to sleep on rocks. Otherwise I might be tempted to take them off even though we could be under attack at any minute," Livia said.

Meikah stared at her boots. She dreaded putting them on after wearing them for so many hours.

"Can I put the light out yet? I want to sleep," Livia said.

Meikah lay down, leaving her boots off. "Yeah. Put it out." She closed her eyes a second before the lantern went out. She was asleep minutes after that, woken hours later by Rafe touching her on the shoulder and whispering her name.

"What's wrong?"

"Dawn is coming."

Chapter Twelve

Meikah sat up, trying to see Rafe in the darkness. She reached blindly for him, not surprised when he took hold of her hand. "Did anything happen while I slept?"

"It was quiet. There were a few sentient zombies out there, but they didn't come close."

"I always thought sentient zombies were peaceful." Meikah drew her hand from his.

"It depends on how they are raised," Kellan said.

She looked in Kellan's direction, wondering how well he could see. "What do you mean?"

"The will of the one who raised them has been forced upon them. It overrides their own desires and can go against the choices they want to make."

"It's wrong," Livia said. "Like they've enslaved someone. Worse than raising spirits or non sentient zombies."

"Why would they do it?" Meikah looked towards Livia, wishing she could see. Being the only one who couldn't was annoying.

"Might be all they can raise," Livia said. "Being a necromancer doesn't mean you can raise all the dead. Some can only raise spirits, some the newly dead."

"Some can raise all," Kellan said.

Rafe took hold of Meikah's hand again, pressing a key into it. "Can you chain the coffin once I'm in it? The sun is only minutes from rising."

"I can barely see anything."

"Livia can open the shutters once I'm in the coffin. Or she could turn on one of the lanterns." Rafe let go of her hand.

She listened as he moved away. Less than a minute later, light entered the loft through the windows Livia had unshuttered. Meikah crossed the room to the coffin, threading the chain through the handles and criss-crossing it over the top to snap the lock into place. Turning the key, she locked it then pocketed the key.

"We might want to close the place up again." Livia remained at one of the windows, looking outside.

Kellan joined her. "Suri did warn us they come in the day." He faced Meikah. "Ready for a fight? It looks like sentient zombies."

Meikah pulled on her boots and gathered her weapons, tying on her mask. "Spirits are easier to fight." A single mortal wound and they were gone. It took more effort to sever the head from a zombie's body.

Livia gathered her weapons and put on her mask before she strode towards the trapdoor and ladder. "We need to find out if the necro has sent spirits or non-sentient zombies. We might be able to figure out who they are if all they can raise are the newly dead."

Meikah followed. "How?"

"By asking the gossips." Kellan finished putting on his mask. "They tend to know everything that's going on in an area."

Meikah wondered what the gossips of Dreyton were saying. She'd probably find out as soon as she arrived home. Her father was likely to complain. After clambering down the ladder she stepped outside, seeing Suri and Flint running towards the zombies, weapons out.

"The zombies could have waited until after breakfast," Livia muttered. She ran towards the horde, changing forms mid stride, streaking past the assassins.

Meikah drew her sword and dagger, lightning

racing along the blades. A glance at Kellan showed he'd also drawn his weapons, continuing to stride towards the zombies.

Two zombies ran towards her, breaking away from the horde that attacked Flint and Suri. She raised her sword, blocking the staff one of them used. For a few seconds she expected him to use magic, but he didn't. He continued to expertly swing the staff. She leapt back, the staff missing her by inches. The other zombie came close, wielding two daggers. Meikah sidestepped, nearly colliding with a third zombie that ran at her. Were they the only humans in town? A glance around showed no others planned to join the fight.

There weren't as many zombies as last night, but they were outnumbered. "We should have brought the rest of our group." Meikah blocked an attack.

Kellan fought at her side. "We can't leave our town unprotected. There's enough of us to deal with this."

Another zombie joined those fighting her so she was kept too busy to argue. Lightning flared along her blades, spreading out so it covered her hands and part of her arms. She barely had time to be shocked, the attacking zombies keeping her moving. Would she be able to throw bolts of lightning like Suri had? Or would she end up hurting her companions with her lack of training? She really needed to learn more. She staggered under the attack of another zombie, relieved when Livia leapt on him, driving him to the ground. She spun to face a zombie that tried to come at her from the left, her dagger barely slowing him, even though his expression registered the pain. Bringing up her sword she pulled her dagger from him, lightning flickering across his body as she severed his head. There wasn't time to watch him fall. She spun to face the zombie behind her.

By the time the zombies had been defeated, her arms ached, her body felt drained and she was starving. Which surprised her. Wanting to eat after a battle shouldn't be possible.

Livia stopped beside Meikah, turning human. "We should probably have breakfast in case another lot arrive."

"I hope there isn't another lot today." Meikah looked down at her weapons, both blades in need of cleaning.

"Let's get cleaned up and see what there is to eat around here." Kellan strode towards Suri.

The assassin showed them where they could wash and said she'd organise a meal for them. When Meikah asked why no one had helped fight, Suri explained there were few humans left. They'd stayed close to the intact buildings since most of them had limited fighting skills.

After they'd washed, they joined Suri and Flint in a cottage with a large timber table that had a meagre meal laid out on it.

Suri gestured towards the food. "Supplies are getting low. One of the storage buildings was burned recently."

Kellan poured himself a drink from the jug in the middle of the table. "Has the necromancer sent anything other than the newly dead against you?"

Flint shook his head. "It's always been sentient zombies. I was expecting spirits to eventually be sent, but Suri said there has been none."

"I know who's sending them," Suri said.

Flint turned to her. "When did you find out?"

Suri nodded to Kellan. "I came to the same conclusion and sent a couple of vampires to King's Peak one evening with a message for our captain. A messenger arrived a couple of days ago. I'd planned to tell you this morning after you were rested from your journey, but we were attacked."

"Who is it?" Kellan asked.

"A necromancer that lives further up the mountain is the most likely culprit. He's been there for decades. Urian. Only works for those willing to pay extremely well. Sarette doesn't believe it's him. Said they grew up together. Knew each other before he became a necro and she became a vampire." Suri grinned. "I think they were sweet on each other."

"Has anyone been to see him?" Livia asked.

Suri shook her head. "You have to be desperate to visit him."

Kellan gestured vaguely around them. "I'd say you are desperate. The village is mostly destroyed, some of the villagers have fled to safety, many have died and only a couple of dozen remain. Is he a living necromancer or a spirit?"

"Living, but it doesn't matter. There are dragon nests up there," Suri said.

"The necro must be crazy." Meikah slowly shook her head. No one lived around dragon nesting grounds. They might as well beg to die.

Kellan grinned. "Guess we are too. We'll visit him after we've eaten." He met Meikah's gaze. "The two of us. Livia can guard Rafe." He turned to Suri. "Do you have a map?"

Chapter Thirteen

"Are you crazy?" Meikah rose from the table, stepping away from him. "We'll be killed."

"Of course we won't." Kellan looked to Suri again. "A map?"

"I'll organise one for you. But you might not want to go. The only access is through a narrow ravine, wide enough you could be taken out by archers along the top," Suri said.

"Then how about a couple of shields we can borrow?" Kellan asked.

"Kellan–"

He interrupted Meikah. "We always go to the source. It's the way we do things."

"I'm with Meikah on this," Flint said. "You're crazy. Throwing our lives away isn't part of what we do."

Finished his meal, Kellan rose from the table.

"Danton isn't the only one who always gets the job done. Isn't that why you came to us? To get the job done? Because that's what I plan to do."

Meikah watched Suri and Flint share a look, pretty certain they were telling each other Kellan was crazy, but it'd be a waste of time trying to stop him. She wanted to tell Kellan there was no way she was going, but she couldn't help thinking about his crazy plan with the flagpole. It had worked even though she'd thought it impossible. Did all his crazy plans work? And even if they had previously, that didn't mean they always would.

"I'll get a map for you." Suri rose from the table.

"I'll see what I can do about shields." Flint looked from one to the other. "You do understand you're on your own up there. No one will be coming after you if something goes wrong."

Livia leaned back in her chair. "That's where you're wrong."

With a sharp nod, Flint followed Suri from the room.

Livia glanced at the door before turning her attention to Kellan. "What's the plan?"

Kellan shook his head. "Not here. We'll go back to the stable loft."

The moment all of them had finished eating,

Meikah followed Kellan, Livia at her side. Necromancers, sentient zombies, dragon nests and a narrow ravine. It wasn't a matter of what could go wrong. It was more a case of was it possible for anything to go right. Kellan better have a plan because she doubted they could face all that without one.

Livia moved closer to Meikah as they neared the stable. "Don't look so worried. Kellan is as good at getting us out of trouble as he is at getting us into it."

"It's the getting into trouble part I'm worried about."

Kellan momentarily looked over his shoulder at Meikah's comment, grinning. "That's the fun part."

She looked down at her clothes. No, that was the part where it was possible to die and end up wearing this outfit. Entering the stable, she hurried ahead of Kellan, grabbing his arm before he could ascend the ladder to the loft. "If you're going to keep taking me into death-defying situations, I want a battle outfit."

"This one won't be anywhere near as bad as the last one. I have a plan." He grinned. "And it isn't crazy." He paused a moment. "You'll be lucky to suffer a scratch."

"If I do suffer worse, does that mean you'll get me a battle outfit?"

"Only if you don't deliberately get hurt."

"Why would I want to do that? I'm not the crazy one."

"It's a deal. And if I get you through without a scratch, you have to promise to accompany me somewhere."

"Where?"

Kellan shrugged. "Somewhere. An event like a gala or the theatre or something." He lowered his voice. "You and me."

Her gaze was caught by his. "All right." Her voice was equally soft. "At least now you've got an incentive to keep me in one piece." She started to turn away.

Kellan tugged her back to him. "I always have an incentive to keep you in one piece." He lowered his head.

She pressed her hand against his chest, stepping away from him. "How can I choose between you? The three of us work together."

"Have you thought it might make it difficult that you can't choose or say that you aren't interested in either of us." Kellan pressed a finger to her lips when she started to speak. "Honestly say you aren't interested and actually mean it."

It was impossible to do either. She stepped away

from him, wishing she could do something about the situation. Rafe was right. She liked both of them. Her attention was caught by Livia coming back into the stable and she wondered when she'd left since she'd followed them into the building.

Livia held up a map. "Suri brought us a map and Flint left shields propped against the outside wall." She looked from one to the other. "Ready to sort out a plan?"

Meikah nodded. Going into a death defying situation was looking more appealing than continuing her current conversation. She'd never spent so much time avoiding situations as she had this past week. Somehow she had to finish figuring out her life.

"We'll see if Rafe is awake." Kellan climbed up the ladder, entering the loft to sit beside the coffin. "Can you hear us?"

"Yes." Rafe's voice was muffled.

Meikah crossed the room to sit on the other side of the coffin. Livia remained by the trapdoor.

"Would other vamps be able to hear me?" Kellan asked.

"Coffins tend to muffle sounds. They would have to be in the same room. Possibly in the room above, below or next door, depending on the materials the building is made of," Rafe said.

Livia strode across the room and sat on the edge of the coffin, in the middle between where the chains crossed over the edge. "Then we're fine. No one other than us are in this building. And no one is directly outside."

Kellan spread the map out on top of the coffin, above the chains. "Suri has marked everything on the map for us."

Meikah stared at the neat handwriting that had been added to the map. 'Ravine'. 'Necromancer'. Her gaze was drawn to the dot labelled 'Longview'. "Will we be able to reach the necro before night?"

"What is going on?" Rafe asked.

Kellan briefly explained.

"Are you mad? You're going to get both of you killed," Rafe said.

"We're going to keep them distracted while you and Livia sneak in and take Urian by surprise." Kellan folded up the map.

"How do you expect us to do that?" Livia demanded. "I can't fly like some." She glanced at the coffin.

"By getting up on top of the ravine and taking them out one at a time. Preferably without being noticed. Once it's dark, unlock the coffin and you and Rafe can follow. You'll be able to cover the ground quicker than we can on horseback." Kellan rose to his feet, looking to Meikah. "Give Livia the key."

Meikah shook her head. "Only if Rafe is happy with that plan."

They all looked at the coffin. Rafe remained silent.

Kellan knocked on the lid. "This would be a good time to speak."

"What's the distance?" Rafe asked.

"It'll take us about five hours to ride there. By the time we saddle the horses and grab some supplies that'll get us there about half an hour before dark." Kellan fell silent a moment. "Have you gone back to sleep?"

"Give the key to Livia," Rafe said.

"Are you sure?" Meikah took the key from her pocket, the metal warm in her hand.

"Yes. I can be there in about two hours, maybe less by flying. You'll be able to hold out long enough for me to take out the necromancer."

"You're to keep him alive," Kellan said. "We need to question him."

"Necromancers can never die." There was humour in Rafe's voice.

Chapter Fourteen

Meikah couldn't resist smiling, handing over the key to Livia. "Be careful." She tapped lightly on the coffin lid. "Both of you."

Livia grinned. "Don't get caught."

Kellan returned her grin. "Don't you get caught either." He turned to Meikah. "We leave in half an hour."

Meikah looked down at her clothes. "A pity I don't have something else to wear. I don't want to spend an eternity in this if I die."

"Simple. Don't die." Kellan strode to the ladder. "I'll saddle the horses."

They were ready in less than half an hour, letting Suri and Flint know they were leaving. The two assassins tried once more to talk them out of going.

Kellan swung up into the saddle. A shield hung on

the saddle so it covered most of his leg. "We have a plan. It'll work."

"I hope so." Suri shaded her eyes against the sun as she looked up at Kellan. "There are too few joining our faction each year that we can't afford to lose any."

Meikah mounted her horse, adjusting the shield so it sat right. Kellan better know what he was doing because she wasn't ready to die. Even if she had a battle outfit like those worn by the assassins in front of her, she still wouldn't be ready. She turned the horse to follow Kellan out of town.

The place was silent, the devastation more noticeable in the bright light of day. Some of the buildings had been burned to the ground, others were mostly intact with doors and shutters smashed. The place looked like it'd take years to rebuild. If enough lived through the experience to be able to rebuild.

Kellan didn't speak until they entered the forest, riding abreast on the path. "Keep watch for wild animals. They're more likely to be a problem than bandits this high up in the mountains."

"I hope that comment wasn't meant to be reassuring."

Kellan chuckled. "You're not about to get reassurances from me. Only assurances that this will work."

"You better be right."

"Of course I am. We're going out somewhere once we return to Dreyton. You and me. Alone."

"Only if I make it back unharmed."

"You will. We both will."

She fell silent, her gaze drawn by every sound. Forests used to conjure images of green, tranquillity and the sound of birdsong. No longer. She wouldn't be able to think of forests without thinking of the dangerous creatures hiding in the shadows and the unidentifiable sounds that kept her hand near the hilt of her night blade sword.

"Relax a little. You'll be jumping at your own shadow soon."

"I think I already am."

She continued to remain vigilant, becoming less tense as time passed and they remained unharmed. Whatever made the noises in the forest stayed out of sight. The path took them higher up the mountain, the air becoming cooler. They were almost in the ravine before they noticed it through the tree cover, the towering rocks covered by dense scrub and vines, a clearing in front of it. Meikah drew her horse to a stop. "It looks dark."

"It'll get worse soon. There's not much left of the day."

"I don't count that as either reassuring or assuring."

Kellan held his shield over his head. "Get ready. We're going in."

She wanted to protest. They were going to die. Thinking of Livia and Rafe, both expecting a diversion, she readied her shield. It felt flimsy considering earlier it had looked solid and sturdy. "They'll be able to shoot me in the legs."

"A leg shot is less likely to be mortal. We can have a healer fix that easier than we can have one fix an arrow through the head."

Neither scenario sounded good. "You might want to stop telling me things like that. Or there's a chance I'll turn around and race back to Longview."

"You wouldn't desert me."

She glanced at Kellan, sighing. He was right. She wouldn't desert any of them. How had they become important to her in such a short amount of time? It felt like she'd known them for years, not a week. "I can't promise the horse won't if an arrow hits him."

"The horse has been trained better than that. He'll keep going."

"I don't know if that makes me feel better or worse." Her gaze was caught by movement above. "I think I'm about to find out though."

"Keep your pace steady. We don't want to race

through the ravine. Keep an eye out for somewhere we can hide and they can keep us pinned down."

She stared at Kellan's back, wanting to tell him that didn't sound like a good plan. "All right." He better know what he was doing. An image of Suri and Flint using their powers together filled her mind. She wanted to be able to do that. Lightning crackled along her hand that held the reins. A moment of panic raced through her when she couldn't immediately get rid of it. Why bother? The horse didn't seem to mind and maybe it'd be useful. She looked at the shield she held over her head. How would she get the lightning into it? With a bit of effort, she changed which hand was holding the shield. It didn't take long for the lightning to crackle across the surface. She was surprised when the timber didn't burn.

A thunk drew her attention and she looked ahead to see an arrow in Kellan's shield, mist forming above him to spread out. "What are you doing?"

"If they can't see us, they can't hit us."

"What if that makes them come down here?"

Kellan glanced over his shoulder, grinning at her. "Then they'll be in the same position as us when Livia arrives."

A couple of arrows pierced the mist, landing to the

side of her. "Unless they hit us before Livia gets here." The arrows had been a little too close.

"Not far now. I can see an area we should be able to hide in. I'll let the mist disperse as we reach it so they can see where we are."

"Wouldn't it be better if they couldn't see us?" With the way the shadows were lengthening, she wouldn't be able to see where they were going shortly. Looking upwards she couldn't see past the mist, but the arrows continued to strike the ground, mostly falling ahead of them.

"We want to keep them focused on us." He paused a moment. "Here we go. It looks big enough. You go in first." He grinned at her when she reached the shallow cave. "I wouldn't want to risk you getting scratched."

She rode into the shallow cave, which was barely big enough for both of the horses, and turned to see the mist had separated. A rain of arrows fell behind Kellan as he rode into the cave. "Are you all right?" She couldn't see any wounds, but there'd been a lot of arrows.

"They missed me. With a little help from my magic." He remained on his horse. There wasn't enough space to dismount.

"How long will we have to stay here?" She could

barely see anything. "Can we light the lantern you brought?"

"Soon."

"How soon?" This was as bad as creeping through the Duke's gardens. The last of the feeble light went and she could see nothing. "How do you see in the dark?"

"It's easier to learn how to create bewitched flames."

"When am I going to learn to do that?"

"When we return home. Unless something else comes up."

She sighed. She supposed she was the one who'd argued about coming. "How far is it from here to King's Peak?"

"A few hours from Longview. We'll get the scarf once we've sorted out the necro."

They fell silent, Meikah thinking about all the recent changes in her life. She never could have expected to find herself in such a situation. She had no idea how much time had passed before she heard noises above.

"That sounds like Livia," Kellan said.

"How will we know for certain?"

A dim light sprang to life in the lantern Kellan held

up. "The zombies should be too busy to attack us." He grinned. "How about we find out?"

Chapter Fifteen

Before Meikah could protest, Kellan rode out of the shallow cave. She stared at him in the opening, holding her breath as she waited for an arrow to pierce him. None came. "She's dealt with them?"

Kellan shrugged, the light rocking, shifting the shadows around. "We'll ride on. She'll catch up."

Meikah wanted to protest. She didn't want to meet Urian, but neither did she want to remain in the ravine. She followed Kellan, Livia joining them a few minutes before they reached a cave entrance, remaining in cat form.

"He lives in there?" Meikah gestured towards the darkness. Who lived in a cave? She dismounted to stand beside Kellan who had done the same.

Livia stalked forward, becoming human as she did so. "I guess there's only one way to find out. Hope Rafe did his part."

The tunnel was short, opening into a central cave with four exits leading off it. Two of the exits had wide openings, leading to smaller caves. One showed a timber framed bed, the other a kitchen area with a table and two chairs that looked like they'd been made from fallen branches and sawn timber. The mahogany colour of them gleamed in the firelight from a cooking fire set off to the side. A metal tripod with a pot hanging over the fire had steam rising from it. Behind the table and chairs stood a set of shelves holding crockery and cookware, the furniture all the same style. The other two exits were too narrow to see where they led.

A man had his hands raised and was pressed against the rough stone wall near the exit leading to the kitchen area, looking as young as Sarette and nowhere near old enough to be several decades old, even with his beard. Rafe stood in front of him, both his daggers drawn, flames dancing along the blades.

Rafe glanced at Livia. "Of course I did my part."

Livia grinned at him. "Shouldn't listen into other people's conversations."

Kellan stopped beside Rafe, his gaze on Urian. "Who are you working for?"

"That is none of your business." Flames flickered in Urian's dark eyes.

Rafe took a step towards him. "We're making it our business. Your zombies are killing people."

The flames disappeared from Urian's eyes, surprise momentarily appearing on his face. "I never work for anyone. They ask for an amount of zombies and once I've provided them, our dealings are done. What they do with them has nothing to do with me."

"Don't you care what they use them for?" Meikah demanded.

"What does it matter? People are all the same. There are no heroes. They're all out for themselves. You think anyone's going to thank you for interfering?"

Meikah stared at him. Surely he didn't mean that. "If you didn't hide-"

"You think I wanted this?" His hand made a sweeping motion, encompassing the cave. "I was driven from my home. Attacked and abused because of something I can do, not what I did. I was an apprentice woodworker, younger than you, when I learned what I was capable of." His gaze travelled across each of them. "You all know what I mean. You're necromancers. Why help people? Not a single one would help you."

"Because no one has shown them any different.

Necromancers live down to expectations," Kellan said.

"What choice do they give us?" Urian demanded. "Only one believed in me, but she wouldn't go against her family and stand up for me."

His words reminded Meikah of Isha. Her grandmother had said something similar. "We make our own choices." She wasn't about to let anyone drive her from Dreyton. It was her home. She'd find a way to keep it that way. If she ever left, it'd be her decision, not something she was driven to do.

"Every person we help is one more who knows there are two kinds of necromancers," Livia said.

"It takes time to change perceptions," Kellan said.

"You can't change anything if you aren't given the chance." Urian took a step towards them.

"Don't move," Rafe warned.

The past week replayed through Meikah's mind in flashes. Fighting her first spirit, Kellan taking her to meet Danton, Webb's daughters, Rafe's father wanting him dead, her own grandfather demanding that she didn't shame their family, Isha standing by her and learning about the Assassins Of The Dead. It had been a strange week. She glanced around the cave. But she was glad she'd met her companions. "Sometimes you have to make those chances."

"Sometimes those chances aren't what you expect them to be," Rafe said.

"You're young. What would you know?" Urian continued to look at Meikah.

Meikah grinned. "You're living in a cave. What would you know?"

Urian stared at her for a moment before he nodded. "Why did you come here? I've been raising zombies for decades. None come demanding I stop. None dare. Why do you think I live so close to dragon nesting grounds?" A smile formed. "It keeps away all but the desperate or foolhardy."

"We want you to stop the destruction of Longview," Kellan said.

Urian looked startled. "What do you mean?"

"Your zombies have been sent against the town," Rafe said.

Urian shook his head. "No, they told me their village had a problem with a dragon attacking or they wouldn't have come to see me. I heard the truth in their words. It was nothing about attacking another village."

"Thought you didn't care what they wanted the zombies for," Livia said.

"It doesn't matter how often I tell them I'm not

interested in their affairs, people always tell me. And they told me the truth. I know it."

She felt a moment of sympathy for him. He looked shaken. "They must have lied."

Urian shook his head again. "It's one thing I have a talent for. Hearing truth and lies. They didn't lie. They came to me because of a dragon that was attacking their village."

Rafe lowered his daggers, the flames going out. "Then hear the truth in my words. Most of the townspeople of Longview have been killed."

"Sarette? Does she live?"

Meikah was surprised by the urgency she could hear in Urian's voice. "She was alive when we left, but we don't know what has happened while we've been gone."

Urian was silent a moment. "I need a map of the area."

Kellan took out the map Suri had given them. "How will a map help?"

"I can cast a spell that will locate where the rest of my zombies are." He strode to the table, pushing aside a clothbound book and goblet before spreading it out. He raised one hand, the other he held over the map.

Meikah moved closer, Rafe on one side, Livia and Kellan on the other. When light appeared above the map, she turned to Livia, keeping her voice low. "What is he doing?"

"It's probably some sort of tracking spell."

The light separated into points, shining on the map. Urian waved his hand and the points blinked out, leaving scorch marks behind before they vanished. He faced them. "Each mark is a zombie. What is left of the five hundred I was commissioned to raise."

Meikah moved forward with her companions, her breath drawn in sharply at the amount of marks on the map. "There must be a hundred of them left."

Urian shook his head. "Closer to fifty or sixty."

Words failed her. That was more zombies than they'd faced before reaching Longview. How were they meant to deal with that many? And where had he found so many of the recently deceased?

Rafe pointed to a place on the map. "There seems to be a lot of them here. The rest seem scattered or circling around Longview. Which town came to you wanting zombies raised?"

"Shadow's Fall."

"Another vampire holding?" Rafe asked.

Urian shrugged. "I don't keep up with the affairs of the world." He glanced at the book on the table.

"Where did you get all the recently deceased from?" The question had kept bothering Meikah.

"They brought them to me." Urian shrugged. "I didn't ask. They didn't say."

"Can't you do something to break whatever you did to raise the zombies?" Meikah asked.

"You know very little about necromancers," Urian said.

Meikah smiled wryly. "I only learned I was one a week ago."

Urian stared at her. "No wonder you believe it's possible to remain in your home. You'll learn." He gathered up the map and held it out to Kellan. "Tell Sarette…" He shook his head. "Never mind. Leave before I raise a new army to guard the ravine." He turned his back on them, his fingers running over the cover of the book resting on the table.

Chapter Sixteen

Meikah wanted to say something. Anything. But no words would lift Urian's slumped shoulders or change the sad tone of his voice. "Thank you for your help." He didn't answer and she walked with her companions to the cave exit. She stopped by her horse, glad of the light from the lantern. "What are we going to do now? Return to Longview?"

"Daylight is hours away. We should pay a visit to Shadow's Fall," Rafe said. "There's no point visiting a vampire holding during the day. Not if you want to talk to the head of the village."

"How are we going to find Shadow's Fall? Do any of you know where it is?" She hadn't heard of it before. But that didn't mean anything. She hadn't heard of Longview either.

Kellan handed the lantern to Rafe and unfolded the

map. "I'm guessing it's near where the majority of the zombies are."

Meikah moved closer to stare at the scorch marks. "Shouldn't we deal with the zombies surrounding Longview?" She ran a finger across the map, circling the village.

Kellan folded the map. "If we can get Shadow's Fall to call off the attack we won't need to worry about those ones." He mounted his horse and took the lantern back from Rafe. "We better go before Urian raises another army. With the amount of killing that goes on in these mountains he likely has more than enough bodies to raise."

Meikah mounted her horse, following Kellan into the ravine, unable to resist looking up even though she knew she wouldn't be able to see anything in the darkness.

"I'll go ahead and check for bandits and creatures." Rafe became a bat, flying into the night.

"He'll probably get into trouble. He doesn't know much about being a shapeshifter." Livia changed form mid stride, racing through the ravine, rapidly disappearing out of sight.

Kellan grinned at Meikah. "Finally. Alone again."

She tried to smile, but one wouldn't form. "How are we going to defeat so many zombies? We're heading directly to where the majority of them are. There has to be at least forty of them. Possibly more."

"I'm working on that."

"You better get it figured out before we arrive. I don't want to die." She remained silent when he didn't answer, continually glancing around as they travelled through the ravine and back to the road through the forest.

Livia joined them an hour later, becoming human. "Take the right fork up ahead. Rafe has travelled along it a fair way and it leads in the direction we need to go."

"Where is he?" Meikah asked.

"Went back to searching the road ahead. I'll stay close for a bit. There's a few creatures around here that might rethink attacking if there's three of us." Livia took Kellan's hand he held out and allowed him to swing her onto the back of his horse.

"What kind of creatures?" Meikah peered into the shadows, unable to see anything.

"The really large kind with fangs and claws."

At Livia's words she wished she hadn't asked. "Zombies are suddenly sounding better."

Kellan chuckled. "I'll remind you of that later."

Again they fell silent, not speaking until Rafe swooped in, changing back from a bat. "There's fire ahead. And a scent I don't recognise." He easily kept up with the pace of the horses.

"How far ahead?" Kellan asked.

Rafe shrugged. "I came back as soon as I noticed. I'll see what I can find out."

"No. We should stay together." Vampires and fire weren't a good mix. She didn't want anything to happen to him.

"I can smell smoke," Livia said. "It's faint. About twenty to thirty minutes away. We'll all find out soon enough what's ahead."

Meikah looked to Kellan. "Hope you've figured out what we're going to do."

He grinned. "Don't get caught?"

Livia chuckled, breaking off at Meikah's daggered look.

"You're not helping. There's a horde of zombies, something is burning and an unknown creature is ahead of us." Meikah looked at Kellan again. "What is the plan?"

"Don't get caught is the perfect plan for that," Kellan said.

She glared at him. "You better not get me killed."

Kellan grinned. "I know. You're not dressed for that."

"I don't want to die no matter what I'm wearing."

She spoke again before someone could remind her necromancers couldn't die. "Or lose my body."

"Of course I'm not going to let you die," Kellan said. "You promised to go on an outing with me if you didn't get a scratch on you from seeking out Urian."

"You did?" Rafe asked.

She wasn't sure what she heard in Rafe's tone. She glared at Kellan. "A pity I didn't. Then you'd owe me a battle outfit."

Livia laughed. "Never bet against Kellan. He doesn't lose."

"It was a bet?"

This time she recognised Rafe's tone. It was relief. "Obviously a terrible one."

"Of course it wasn't terrible. You won either way. An evening with me or a battle outfit. How can either of them be considered losing?" Kellan asked.

A smile reluctantly formed. "I wouldn't say that exactly." Her smile faded at the glimpse of light she saw through the trees. "Fire."

"We need to get closer." Kellan urged his horse into a canter.

Meikah followed, not wanting to be left behind in the dark, Rafe running beside her horse. The smell of smoke grew stronger and the flames brighter. They came out of the forest at the edge of a village that was on fire. It didn't look like the first time the place had burned. Many of the buildings were charred remains. Some of the buildings, which were currently alight, looked like they'd been burned before while some had flames dancing across mostly untouched timber.

Villagers called out, tossing buckets of water over flames that came back instantly. A handful of archers, who had been watching the sky, turned their bows towards Meikah and her companions.

Kellan raised his hands. "Lower your weapons and I'll call rain to put out the fire."

The villagers kept their bows aimed at them. "Either help or return the way you came," one of the archers ordered.

Meikah caught a glimpse of canines when he spoke.

Kellan grinned. "Do you really think I'm going to want to help when you might accidentally shoot one of us?" Mist formed above him.

The archer, who'd spoken, lowered his bow. He gestured to those with him to do the same. "Hurry up then."

Kellan sent the mist towards the burning buildings, rain falling when it reached them. The moment the flames were out, bewitched flames flickered to life in several metal lampposts, the glass gone, and in the windows of a couple of nearby buildings. Kellan faced the archer. "What is going on here?"

"That is none of your business. You've put the fire out, now you can be on your way," the archer said. "We're not about to trust anyone who hides their face with a mask."

"Why are you attacking Longview?" Livia asked.

Arrows were drawn back again and aimed at them. "Sarette sent you?" the archer demanded.

"Should have shot them on sight," one of the archers said, his words filled with anger.

Kellan drew his medallion out to let it hang against his shirt, the leather cord around his neck. Seeing Livia do the same, Meikah drew hers out, Rafe drawing his out too.

The archer lowered his bow again. "You come from the king?"

His words startled Meikah and she wanted to ask what he meant. But there'd be no whispering questions around here. The vampires would hear.

"Why don't you answer the question my friend asked?" Kellan gestured towards Livia. "Why did you attack Longview?"

Before the archer could answer, there was a roar in the sky, wings beating as a large shape came in fast. Flames poured from an open mouth to set fire to several buildings as it flew past. Firelight reflected off dark green scales.

Rafe drew his daggers, flames racing across the blades.

Kellan held up a hand. "Don't attack. Dragons have long memories and never forget a scent." He turned his horse. "Go. Now." He raced towards the forest, the dragon coming around for another attack.

Chapter Seventeen

Meikah followed Kellan. Rafe remained at her side, continuing to hold his daggers. Around them villagers called out, racing towards the forest, some in a blur, others at human speed, a few carried by vampires. Meikah couldn't resist constantly checking over her shoulder. The dragon didn't follow. She doubted it could with how close the trees were.

"Looks like Urian was right," Livia said when they came to a stop, holding the lit lantern. "They're having dragon problems."

The archer stepped out of the shadows, two vampires following him. "It's Sarette's fault. If it wasn't for her sorcerer the dragon wouldn't be trying to kill us."

"What did she do?" Meikah asked.

A vampire rushed up to the archer before he could speak. "The dragon has gone."

The archer nodded. "Tell everyone to return to putting the fire out." He looked at Kellan. "I don't have time for your questions."

"I'll put out the fire if you answer our questions," Kellan said.

Meikah wanted to protest. Surely he wouldn't let the houses burn.

After a moment, the archer nodded. "As long as you tell me why you have a vampire in your ranks." He glanced towards Rafe. "I've never heard of a vampire working for the King before."

"It's a deal," Kellan said.

With another nod, the archer turned and headed back to the village in a blur of movement. They followed him, Kellan and Livia dismounting before he raised the mist, sending it towards the fires, the rain putting out the flames. Lowering his hands, Kellan leaned against Livia, slipping an arm around her waist.

Meikah dismounted, moving closer to Kellan, Rafe coming to stand beside her.

"You owe us some answers," Kellan said. "How about we start with who you are."

The archer nodded. "Larkin. This is my village. Or what's left of it." He glanced at Rafe. "Now tell me why you have a vampire with you."

"You haven't answered all our questions," Kellan said. "Why are you attacking Sarette and how can the dragon attacks be her fault?"

Several vampires came forward with stools for them to sit on. Rafe declined, standing at Meikah's shoulder when everyone sat. Two vampires stood behind Larkin.

"I'd invite you inside, but the buildings are a death trap of an evening. She only attacks at night. Nothing we do will appease her," Larkin said.

His words had Meikah glancing towards the sky. The dragon wasn't in sight. They were safe for now. Her gaze was drawn back to Larkin. She hoped they were safe. "What does the dragon want?"

"Her egg," Larkin said.

"Start at the beginning." Kellan continued to lean against Livia, his arm around her waist, as hers was around his.

Meikah could see the fatigue, but assumed those who didn't know him wouldn't notice the subtle differences. She planned to ask him later why he'd chosen to lean on Livia rather than her.

"Sarette sent her sorcerer to our village during the day, telling her to find someone willing to go after a dragon's egg. I wouldn't have thought any of my people to be that stupid." Larkin slowly shook his head. "Apparently one was."

"Wasn't stupid. He was greedy. Thought the sorcerer would keep her word when she said she could mask the scent of the egg on him so the mother wouldn't come after him in revenge," one of the vampires standing behind Larkin said.

"Should have demanded the sorcerer also mask the scent of where the egg was taken. His house was the first to go. Him in it," the other vampire said.

"Are you sure it was Sarette?" Rafe asked. "Would the egg smell anything like a dragon?"

Larkin nodded. "They have a similar scent."

"Tonight was the first time I've ever come across the scent of a dragon." Rafe gestured towards the sky. "I didn't notice that scent at Longview."

"She must have taken it somewhere else," Larkin said.

"Why would she need a dragon egg?" Livia asked.

"Her sorcerer is going to make a potion so she can walk about in the day," Larkin said.

"It isn't right," one of the vampires behind Larkin said. "It's unnatural. Does she want more humans to come after us? Many don't tolerate us as it is. This would have most of the country hunting us down."

Rafe shook his head. "Impossible. No such potion exists."

Larkin shrugged. "That's what I thought, but the sorcerer swore she could make such a potion."

"Is that why you sent zombies to kill everyone?" Kellan asked.

"Obviously the dragon can't smell her egg at Longview. If we can't safely live here, then we'll take Sarette's holding as our own. She owes us for what her sorcerer did."

"The sorcerer must be powerful if she can hide a dragon egg from its mother," Livia said.

Larkin shrugged again. "All I know is that dragon thinks we're to blame and that we have the egg. I know for a fact it isn't here. We've turned the place upside down looking for it. And the neighbours of the idiot who stole it said they saw him hand over something large enough to be an egg to a robed woman the day before the dragon attacked. It was covered by an old blanket."

Kellan stood, Livia rising with him. "We need to talk to Sarette and find out exactly what is going on." He held Larkin's gaze for a moment. "And you need to end the attacks until we get to the bottom of everything."

Larkin rose from his stool, taking a step towards

Kellan. "You can't stop me from going after her. She deserves to die for what she's done. Her and all her people."

"Give us a week." Kellan touched the medallion that continued to rest against his shirt. "You want the King to learn you attacked someone working on his behalf?"

"A day."

"Ridiculous. Nothing can be done in so little time. Six days."

Meikah listened to them argue back and forth, wanting to interrupt and tell Larkin that daylight was only a couple of hours away and they needed to get Rafe somewhere safe before then. Eventually a truce was agreed upon. They had until the sun set three times. If nothing was sorted, the rest of the zombies would be sent against Longview when the sun set on the third day. It didn't seem like enough time to Meikah.

"Now why do you have a vampire with you?" Larkin demanded.

Kellan grinned. "His people didn't want him, but we did. His talents are useful to the King."

Meikah could see Larkin wasn't impressed with the answer. She was glad to leave before he decided to do something about it.

The first part of the journey back to Longview was silent. It wasn't until they were well away that Meikah asked what Larkin had meant about them being from the King.

Kellan tucked the medallion beneath his shirt, Livia having already put hers away. "It's one of the King's seals. Why else do you think people give us so much respect? The majority of people don't know about the Assassins Of The Dead, but many recognise the King's seals."

"What if someone made a copy?" Meikah asked.

"They'd be hunted down and killed. No one is allowed to make a copy of any of the King's seals. Not the ones he gives his spies or the ones he gives his high ranking officials. And especially not the ones he gives us."

She tucked her medallion out of sight, noticing that Rafe did the same. "I didn't realise. I thought it was something our faction created."

"In a way it is. But the King is the one who claims it as one of his seals for his people."

Meikah had no idea how to reply. She was one of the King's people? He was the King and as such they were all his people. Having one of his seals, like he approved of her, was strange. A smile formed. Harlen would be jealous if he was to ever find out. It was a pity she couldn't let him know.

"What's so amusing?" Kellan asked.

Chapter Eighteen

Meikah shook her head, not wishing to share her petty thought with Kellan. She turned to Rafe. "You should go ahead without us. Livia too. You don't want to be caught out in the sun and someone needs to make sure your coffin is secure."

Livia was seated behind Kellan. "Are you all right to ride by yourself? Maybe Meikah should ride behind you to keep you from falling off your horse."

"I'll be fine." Kellan grinned, but it appeared to be forced. "Go before Rafe ends up as a pile of ash."

When Livia and Rafe had left, one flying and the other running in cat form, Meikah rode closer to Kellan. "Are you sure you'll be fine? I can ride with you."

"What was I thinking? I should have begged you to ride with me. It's not often I have the chance to be that close to you."

She rolled her eyes. "For that comment I'm going to let you fall on the ground and keep riding without a backwards glance."

"Heartless." Kellan ruined his reply by grinning.

"Why did you lean on Livia instead of me, earlier?"

"I didn't want to risk you telling me to let you go. I wasn't about to explain why. Not with how well vampires can hear. Livia and I have worked together for a while. She knows my limitations."

"And you reached them today?"

"It's difficult pulling moisture from the air when there's none in the area. I had to draw it from further away."

"Oh." She paused a moment. "I wouldn't have pulled away. I didn't know how much effort it took, but I could see how fatigued you were. The vampires probably didn't know, but I did."

Kellan reached out to brush his hand across her arm, meeting her gaze for a moment before he lowered his hand. They continued on in silence, daylight creeping into the sky, shadows continuing to fill the forest.

After they'd ridden in silence for a while, Meikah said, "I'm glad we're not far off reaching Longview. I'm tired and hungry. Being awake all night is starting to become a habit."

"Next time it could be early mornings. You never know what might happen from one job to the next."

Before Meikah could ask Kellan about previous jobs, four bandits burst through the trees to stop in front of them. They were mounted, two with swords, the other two holding bows. One of the bandits that held a sword urged his horse forward a couple of paces. "Dismount. Then throw down your weapons and valuables."

Meikah could only stare at them. Bandits had been the last thing she'd expected, especially after being in a dragon attack.

Kellan remained astride his horse. He glanced at Meikah. "They're lucky they didn't stumble across us earlier. Livia would have torn their throats out."

"Get off your horses now!" the same bandit yelled at them. "Before I tell my friends to fire."

Kellan grinned. "You don't want to do that. How about I give you a chance. Let you run while you can." Tendrils of mist began to form behind him.

Meikah wanted to protest. Kellan was already exhausted. What would happen if he continued to use his magic? "I think you should be the ones to drop your weapons." Seeing the flicker of surprise in their expressions, she drew her sword and urged the horse forward. Lightning crawled along the blade as she advanced on the bandit to the right. One that had a bow pointed at them. The rush of the arrow passed by her cheek a moment before she attacked.

The bowman dropped his weapon, drawing a dagger, his horse rearing before he could attack. One of the sword wielding bandits came at her, yelling as he swung his sword.

She met the attack, drawing back her sword to strike at him. Off to her side she heard the clash of metal and threats. The bandit parried her blow, coming in for another attack, the bowman on his feet and running at her with his dagger. There wasn't time to block both. Not while she was on horseback.

A growl was followed by a streak of black coming through the forest to leap on the bowman, Livia pinning him to the ground in cat form. The bowman screamed, dropping his dagger as he put up his arms to protect his face.

Meikah blocked the swordsman who turned away to attack Livia. She raised her hand, fear racing through her as the sword came closer to Livia's black pelt. "No!" Lightning spread out from her fingers and palm, forking across the air in a crack of thunder, striking the bandit who dropped to the ground, unmoving.

Everyone froze.

A different kind of fear raced through Meikah. Had she killed him? Her stomach lurched as she staggered forward, checking his pulse. It felt wrong to kill with magic. It went against years of templar training. Not just from the academy, but from her parents and grandparents too. She found a pulse. Weak and thready. Her legs nearly gave way at the relief of finding him alive.

Livia backed away from the man she'd pinned to the ground, becoming human as she did so. "I suggest you grab your friend and go." She barred her teeth. "Before I change my mind and tear your throats out."

Meikah rose to her feet, taking a step away from the bandit. She spun when she saw movement at the corner of her eye, finding Kellan moving close to her. He looked worse than before. She slipped an arm around his waist, worried he might collapse.

The bandit that had told them to throw down their weapons picked up his unconscious companion. "This is our territory. If you stay in the area, we'll come after you and finish the job next time."

Livia laughed, slowly stalking him. "That will work as well as this time." She pointed a finger at him. "I suggest you leave the area." She kept up a slow and steady pace, advancing as he retreated. "If I see you around here again, I will tear your throat out." A low rumbling growl rose from her throat. "And enjoy every second of it."

Meikah wanted to protest, but Livia's words had the desired result. The bandits gathered their weapons and horses and rode off, the unconscious one slung over his saddle. She turned to Kellan. "Are you all right?"

He leaned more heavily on her. "I've been better."

Livia rushed to his side, slipping an arm around his waist so that she brushed against Meikah's arm. "You look like we're going to need to sling you over the back of your horse like the bandits did to their companion that Meikah took out."

"I have no idea how I did that." Meikah helped Livia get Kellan to his horse.

Kellan struggled to swing himself into the saddle. His efforts almost ended in him sliding off again. "Danton was right. You need to practice."

Livia leapt onto the back of Kellan's horse, holding him upright. "She can practice when we return to Dreyton. Right now, we have to find out what Sarette has been up to."

Meikah gathered the reins of the horse, sheathing her sword before she swung into the saddle. "Thank you for coming back."

"You didn't think I'd leave you to find your way

to Longview on your own." Livia urged the horse forward.

Meikah rode beside Livia and Kellan. "I didn't think you'd be back before we arrived at Longview." She hesitated a moment. "Could I have killed him? With my lightning."

"If you'd continued to strike him with it." Kellan frowned. "That bothers you?"

"In a way." She shrugged. "I'm used to using a sword. Magic feels unnatural."

"It didn't seem that way," Livia said. "The way you threw that lightning at him, it looked like you'd been doing it for years."

"It would be nice if I could figure out how I did it." She smiled wryly. "Actually, it'd be nice if I could figure out any of this."

"Give it time." Livia momentarily smiled at Meikah before becoming serious. "We need to pick up the pace before Kellan falls off his horse."

"I'm not about to fall off." His words were slurred.

They ignored him, increasing their speed and remaining silent for the rest of the journey. It didn't take long to reach Longview. The village was silent and they rode to the stable where they helped Kellan off the horse and up the ladder.

Chapter Nineteen

Once Kellan was lying on a pallet, Meikah tapped on the lid of the coffin. "We're back." She would tell Rafe about the bandits later. He didn't need to know when he was trying to sleep.

"Sarette will be sleeping, but the humans will be awake. See if one of them knows about the sorcerer," Rafe said.

Kellan raised himself up on an elbow. "Not now. You both need sleep too." A grin fleetingly appeared. "Or you'll be the ones collapsing."

"I can-" Livia began.

Kellan interrupted her. "No. We have enough time. Sleep. No need to keep watch while there's a truce. If anyone comes up the ladder we'll hear them."

Meikah felt like she should argue, but she was too tired to think. She was also too tired to eat even though she was hungry. "All right. I'll have a couple of hours sleep before I see if anyone knows where I can find the sorcerer."

She'd barely stretched out on the pallet when she was asleep, waking later than she'd planned, the sound of someone entering the loft causing her to reach for her dagger. She placed the weapon back on the floor beside her when she saw it was Suri. "Is something wrong?"

Kellan and Livia had also woken, both now lowering their weapons. Livia opened the shutters to let in more light. "Has Shadow's Fall broken the truce?"

Suri shook her head. "I'm afraid it's about to be the other way around. The handful of humans that had survived want to go after Shadow's Fall. They're determined to take revenge for those they've lost. Even though most of them aren't capable of fighting."

"What did Livia tell you when she brought Rafe back?" Kellan asked.

"Very little. That you'd learned Shadow's Fall are the ones attacking and we have a short truce. Why did they agree to a truce? What is going on?" Suri asked.

Kellan stretched, rising to his feet. "Organise breakfast and we'll tell you and Flint at the same time."

Suri left with a nod.

Meikah stared after her. How were they going to stop Longview from attacking Shadow's Fall? Besides being outnumbered, it wouldn't solve anything. They needed to figure out exactly what was going on. Before something else went wrong.

"What is happening?" Rafe's voice was muffled. "Why is everyone quiet?"

Meikah tugged at the mask she was unaccustomed to wearing all the time. "Trying to figure out what to do next."

Kellan spoke at the same time as Meikah. "Wondering if Flint and Suri would come looking for us if we had another hours' sleep."

Livia chuckled. "I'm sure they would." She tapped on the coffin as she passed it. "We'll be back at sunset to let you out."

"Don't get caught," Rafe said.

Kellan grinned. "Of course not." He headed for the ladder. "The first thing I'm going to do when we get to King's Peak is have a feast. We should have brought more supplies."

"I can go hunting," Livia offered.

Meikah followed them down the ladder and to the cottage Flint and Suri were staying in. The meal was as meagre as last time, Flint and Suri rising from the table when they entered. She dreaded the coming conversation. Would they leave Longview to their fate if Sarette was at fault? It didn't seem fair that her people should pay for her crimes.

Once they were seated Kellan told Suri and Flint what they'd learned, between mouthfuls, and answered their many questions. Silence filled the cottage, Flint and Suri sharing a look.

Suri pushed her plate away, resting her arms on the table. "There's no sorcerer here. Maybe it was a necro using Sarette as a scapegoat. Although why they'd want a dragon's egg I don't know."

"What about the humans? Would they know anything?" Meikah asked. She didn't want to wait until sunset. They had little enough time to deal with everything.

Suri shrugged. "We can ask. But no one seems to do anything around here without Sarette's permission. Which is why I was surprised they were going to attack Shadow's Fall without her say so."

Meikah joined Suri as she strode around the village, seeking out the handful of humans remaining. Each said the same. 'You'll have to ask Sarette.' After hearing it for the fifth time, Meikah nearly growled in frustration, but at least the villagers now seemed less inclined to attack Shadow's Fall.

"You must know if there's a sorcerer here. Longview isn't that big a place." Meikah didn't bother keeping the annoyance from her voice.

The villager glanced away, giving another shrug. "Sarette will be awake in an hour."

Meikah took a deep breath. "Surely you know who lives here. Or lived here."

The villager shrugged again. "A lot of people died."

Her hands tightened into fists and she forced herself to open them, trying desperately to remain calm when she felt the power rise in her. "What is the sorcerer's name?"

The villager took a step backwards, fear flaring in his eyes. "Talk to Sarette." Another step backwards. "She knows everything." The villager looked everywhere but at Meikah.

She strode away before she gave into the urge to shake the villager. Was a name too much to ask for? Her gaze was drawn skywards, the sun low on the horizon, the shadows lengthening.

"It's been like this the entire time. No one wants to say or do anything without Sarette's permission." Suri walked beside her.

"Are they scared of her?"

Suri shook her head. "They're scared, but not of Sarette. Or at least not directly scared of her. They're hoping she can save them. This is their home and they don't want to do anything that might make her send them away."

She could understand that fear. She wouldn't want to lose her home either. "Don't they understand we're trying to help them?"

"You're not a vampire. They don't trust you."

Meikah's gaze followed one of the villagers who'd changed direction when she'd seen them coming towards her. "They aren't vampires."

"Most of them want to be. They hope that by serving a vampire master they'll eventually be turned." Suri was silent a moment. "We'll talk to Sarette when she wakes." With a nod, Suri strode away.

Meikah stopped, watching Suri head back to the cottage. How could the assassin sound so calm? Wasn't she annoyed that the villagers weren't willing to cooperate? How were they meant to save Longview if they weren't going to give them the information they needed?

Kellan came towards her. "Any luck?"

"No."

He grinned. "Don't take it personally." Reaching her side, he draped an arm around her shoulders.

"Livia went hunting. We've got a couple of humans cooking a pig on a spit for us. Tonight we eat well."

She walked beside him towards the stable, her mouth watering. "Next time we go somewhere we take plenty of supplies."

"Next time." He repeated her words, grinning. "This hasn't changed your mind about being in our faction?" He lowered his arm, stepping back to let her go up the ladder to the loft.

She met his gaze for a moment. "Maybe I should learn a few things first." Like throwing lightning when she meant it, not accidentally. That was likely to get someone killed. Such as one of her companions.

"We'll see who's available to train you. Although if you get Amiel on your side there's a lot he can teach you about being a necromancer."

"Amiel? But I don't want to learn how to raise the dead."

"He knows a lot more than that." Kellan gestured towards the ladder. "You going up?"

"I suppose I should, before it gets too dark to see properly." She didn't want to fall off the ladder. The closest healer was probably at King's Peak. If she was lucky.

Livia was closing the shutters as Meikah entered the

loft, turning the lantern on when Meikah stumbled in the darkened area. "Sorry. You're really going to have to learn how to see in the dark." When there was a knock from inside the coffin, Livia turned towards it. "The sun isn't set yet. Do you really want to come out before it does?"

"It's as good as set." Kellan entered the loft. "None of us are likely to open the shutters."

"I'll wait," Rafe said.

Livia unlocked the padlock, removing the chains to let them fall on the floorboards beside the coffin. "Another five minutes or so and you can come out." She turned to Meikah. "Did you learn anything?"

Chapter Twenty

Meikah wished she had better news for Livia. "I learned that the people of Longview don't do anything without Sarette's permission."

Kellan chuckled. "You don't sound impressed."

"We don't have the time to waste. Maybe Larkin is right. Sarette might be behind everything. Why else wouldn't her people talk?" Meikah asked.

"Because they don't want to interfere with any of her plans." Rafe shifted the lid of the coffin to the side, sitting up to meet Meikah's gaze. "A head vampire's word is law. No matter what. But I had thought they might give you the information since Sarette accepted our help."

Meikah breathed out heavily. "Well it's frustrating. There are only two sunsets left now." If someone had talked, they might have already found the sorcerer and convinced her to return the dragon egg. She didn't know if that would stop the dragon trying to kill everyone, but it was worth a try.

Rafe stepped out of the coffin. "Sarette should be awake now."

Meikah's hand went to the hilt of her sword. "Then let's ask her what's going on."

Livia's lips curved into a smile, her eyes darkening, filling with shadows. "My favourite part of a mission. Making them talk."

"She's not the enemy," Kellan said. "Not yet."

"If she's the one who started all of this, she will regret it," Livia stated.

Meikah began to ask Livia what she planned to do, but they didn't have time. There were questions to ask and answers to find before the sun rose and Sarette retired for the day. She grabbed the lantern. "It's much easier doing this by daylight."

Kellan followed her to the ladder. "It's much easier finding things out when hidden by shadows."

"Night is when things happen in a vampire holding." Rafe waited until they were down the ladder, dropping through the opening to land beside them.

Meikah strode outside, Kellan next to her, Livia on the other side of Kellan. Rafe walked silently on her left. Taking a deep breath, she headed towards the building Rafe gestured towards, determined to find answers. Too many people had died. In both villages.

Vampires stepped forward to block their way when they entered Sarette's house, one of them Devin. Sarette waved them aside, seated at a table, a goblet in front of her. "Let them through. They have questions."

Meikah didn't bother asking how Sarette knew. She spotted a couple of the humans she'd talked to earlier. "We need to speak to your sorcerer." She stopped in front of the table, her companions beside her.

"I have no sorcerer. We offered refuge to a woman who said she had a limited ability in potion making. She was escaping an arranged marriage. Naren was one of the first to die in the attacks. She didn't stand a chance. There must have been thirty zombies that attacked her. The rest of us faced about a hundred between us. But not her. They were determined to kill her. Tell me what you learned." Sarette topped up her goblet from the bottle on the table, a dark red liquid filling it to the brim. Gesturing a human forward with second cup, she filled it too. "I've only heard bits and pieces from my people. What they managed to work out from your questions."

"Naren told one of the villagers from Shadow's Fall

that she was making a potion to allow you to walk in the daylight," Meikah said.

"She lied." Sarette took a sip from the second goblet before holding it out to Rafe. "There is no such thing as a potion to allow a vampire to walk in daylight." She looked at each of them. "And if there was, I wouldn't be foolish enough to let it be made. It'd be suicidal."

Rafe sipped from the goblet. "You'd need a larger holding than this for such an endeavour."

Sarette nodded. "Exactly." She looked to Meikah. "I don't know what Naren was up to, but I can show you the remains of the cottage she lived in." Rising, she gestured for Meikah to go ahead. She was dressed differently to the previous day. Her clothes were a mixture of silk, lace, velvet and leather, a corset laced up over her long sleeved black shirt. She wore a skirt over her trousers, gathered and layered at the back, open at the front to show her trousers and black boots. And her hair hung down her back.

Meikah held Sarette's gaze a moment, nodding and leading the way outside, continuing to carry the lantern. She stopped in front of the doorway, not knowing where to go.

"This way." Sarette headed to the left, three

vampires following her. Several humans remained at a distance as they too followed.

Meikah hurried forward to walk at Sarette's side, the lantern swinging back and forth to send shadows dancing across the ground. "Why would someone who can make potions need a dragon's egg?"

Sarette shrugged, reaching the edge of town to stop in front of a burnt house frame. "This was her cottage."

A robed, hooded figure stepped out of the shadows. "Longevity Potion."

Sarette waved her people away. "Urian."

He pushed his hood back, making a sweeping gesture that indicated the village. "I didn't know."

Sarette nodded. "You look well."

Urian inclined his head. "Even amidst all of this you look untouched by the troubles that would effect anyone else."

Sarette laughed softly. "I don't know about that, but send what they will, no one will take Longview from me." She held out her hand.

Urian stepped forward, bringing it to his lips. "Can I raise an army to help you protect what is left?"

"No. Let the dead rest. They fought fiercely to protect the holding." Sarette drew her hand from

Urian's. "I appreciate you leaving your mountain retreat to visit me."

Meikah gestured towards the burnt dwelling. "What are we going to do about this?" It was easy to see there was nothing that remained of Naren or the dragon egg. "How are we going to convince the dragon to leave Shadow's Fall alone?"

"Without the egg, the only option is to kill the dragon," Urian said. "They never forget and never forgive. Being law abiding citizens you might not wish to break the King's law."

Not liking the mocking tone of Urian's last comment, Meikah started to demand what other options they had. She didn't get the chance.

Livia stepped closer to the burnt building. "Something is alive in there." She breathed in deeply. "I can smell nothing other than the scent of the charcoal and smoke, but I can hear something else. It's faint."

Rafe joined Livia, frowning. "There might be a heartbeat. Below the ground. Are there tunnels beneath Longview?" He turned to Sarette.

It was Devin who answered. "A cellar. Many of these cottages have cellars for storing food." He gestured several humans forward. "Find the entrance."

Meikah watched the villagers come forward to move half burnt beams, a couple more scurried away returning shortly with various tools. She turned to Sarette. "Can we help?"

Sarette shook her head. "Leave them to their task." She faced Urian. "Would you join me for the evening meal?"

"I need to return home." Urian took Sarette's hand again. "It was good to see you."

"It's been too long." Sarette remained where she was, watching as Urian strode away, drawing up his hood. When he was well out of sight, she turned to Meikah and her companions. "Dinner is ready. We appreciate that you went hunting earlier." She walked away before anyone could speak.

Meikah glanced at the villagers, who continued to work, before turning to Kellan. "We don't have time to sit around eating. We need to figure everything out."

Flint joined them. "I'm travelling to King's Peak at daylight to inform my captain about what is happening here. Do you want me to take a letter to be sent on to Danton?"

"Yes." Kellan turned to Meikah. "We need to eat. I'll scribble a note to Danton and join you shortly. We can't do much else until the cellar is found."

Chapter Twenty-One

Meikah wanted to argue with Kellan. Surely there was something that could be done. Anything. They were wasting time. And they had so little of it to waste.

Rafe draped an arm around Meikah's shoulders. "Food then we'll return here to see what the villagers might have found."

"I'm starving even if you aren't. I haven't had a decent feed since we arrived." Livia grinned. "You don't want me looking at the villagers like they might be my next meal."

Breathing out heavily, Meikah nodded. "As soon as we've eaten we'll return here."

Kellan grinned. "Don't get caught." He strode towards the stable.

Meikah walked beside Rafe, his arm remaining

around her shoulders, Livia on the other side of her. "How long can a dragon egg last without warmth?"

"We don't know that it is a dragon egg," Livia said.

"There's not a lot known about dragon eggs. Or dragons. People tend not to steal eggs. The only way to do it safely is to kill the mother. Not an easy task, not to mention now being illegal," Rafe said. "The mother isn't likely to take the scent of her egg from you which means other dragons will also know you've handled an egg."

"How do you know all this?" Meikah asked.

"Our holding isn't far from the Arcton Mountains. You can't live anywhere near them without learning that dragons are to be avoided. And to never anger one. It'll be your last deed. Last night was the first time I've come close to one. The stories I've heard weren't exaggerated." Rafe stepped back so Meikah could enter the door.

She stopped not far inside Sarette's house, surprised to see so much food on the table when only Sarette, Flint and Suri were seated. What about the rest of the villagers? She didn't want them to go without. There was a platter piled high with slices of pork, the scent making her mouth water.

Sarette turned to Devin, gesturing him to her side.

After a murmured conversation, he came towards them.

Rafe draped an arm around Meikah's shoulders again. "Sarette believes there is something wrong. We are here to help. She wouldn't harm any of us. Especially not after all the help we've given them."

Devin reached them, inclining his head towards Rafe. "Your friend is correct. We have no plans to harm any of you."

"That wasn't what I was concerned about." Meikah glanced at Rafe and Livia. "I was worried about taking food that the villagers might need." The pig Livia had caught wouldn't make that big a difference.

Devin glanced over his shoulder to Sarette. "She requests that you talk to her. She would never allow her people to starve."

Meikah strode towards the table, Devin following behind the three of them. "I didn't mean to suggest you'd let anyone starve. I was worried there wouldn't be enough food." Not after how little she'd seen served at previous meals.

Sarette gestured towards the chairs. "Take a seat and set your worries aside. Our problems are nearly solved and I can tell the rest of my people to return. They'll bring supplies with them and we'll rebuild in no time."

Meikah placed the lantern on the table and pulled out one of the chairs, sitting down, Rafe and Livia on either side of her. "We only have two more sunsets to solve everything."

Sarette smiled. "Plenty of time." She gestured towards the food. "Eat. You'll need your strength. I'm sure there'll be plenty that needs to be done between now and the time we have left."

They were partway through the meal, Kellan having joined them and handed a letter to Flint, when two villagers burst into the room. They were smeared with black streaks from charcoal and one of them had singed hair. Coming to a stop by the table, they remained silent, waiting for Sarette to speak.

"What happened?" Sarette asked.

Meikah had barely managed not to ask that exact question, having started to rise from her seat when they'd entered. Rafe had tugged her down.

"There was a trap," the one with the singed hair said. "I was further back than a couple of the others. It was a lightning strike."

The other villager continued the explanation. "We'd barely got the trapdoor into the cellar open when lightning seemed to rise from the ground, striking all those nearby, the air crackling. We lost three people."

Sarette stared at the villagers for a moment before she spoke. "See that they are taken care of and notify any family that might live." She rose from the table. "Has anyone entered the cellar?"

The first villager nodded. "Only to the bottom of the stairs. No one dared go any further. We expected another trap."

"Was there anything in the cellar?" Meikah asked.

The villager shrugged. "It was dark. Like night had been left in there. A lantern didn't help."

Kellan rose to his feet, the rest of them doing the same. "What was Naren? If she did the spell in the cellar, she was more than someone who knew how to make potions."

"That is what I would like to know." Sarette strode towards the door, her people hurrying after her.

Meikah stepped in front of Kellan, preventing him from following Sarette. "What spell is it?"

It was Livia who answered. "A sleep spell."

"That doesn't sound too bad." Meikah had been expecting something worse. Maybe a poisonous cloud or something similar.

"A sleep so deep you can't be woken while you're in it. And no one can drag you from it because if they entered the area of the spell it would send them to sleep too. Even if they only partially entered," Kellan said.

Meikah looked from Kellan to Livia. "How are we meant to discover what it's hiding?"

Livia's mouth dropped open, a soft sound escaping. "That's why the dragon can't find her egg. No one can see past a sleep spell. It's impossible."

"We need to get to Naren's home," Rafe said. "They're discussing what to do."

Meikah grabbed the lantern off the table before they hurried through the deserted streets, all the villagers seeming to be gathered around Naren's home. There were eight left. Sarette stood at the top of the stairs, looking into the darkness.

"Can vampires see into a sleep spell?" Meikah asked.

"No one," Livia repeated. "Not even vampires."

Meikah wanted to ask what Sarette was doing. She frowned. "If Naren can make such powerful spells like the sleep spell and the lightning trap, why didn't she use her spells to help her fight the zombies? None of you believed her to be a sorcerer so I'm guessing she didn't."

Sarette faced Meikah. "That's a very good question." She glanced around at her people. "Did anyone see her use spells while fighting for her life?"

Some of the villagers shook their head, others said no. One woman stepped forward. "I lived next door to her and never once saw her use magic. She frequently had potions brewing, but nothing else."

"You'd think she'd use magic if her life was in that much danger," Livia said.

"So she couldn't use magic." Meikah's gaze was drawn to the open trapdoor. "She either used a scroll that if it was here would have been destroyed and the spell would be gone or an object empowered with the spell."

"Has to have been an object," Livia said. "It'd be too costly to use scrolls. You'd need a new one each time you wanted to get rid of the spell and put it back in place."

"She'd want it nearby so she could speak the words to raise and lower the spells when she wanted to enter the cellar," Kellan said.

Meikah glanced around. "How will we know what it is? Anything could have been used."

"Normally it's something small," Rafe said. "With the words of the spell engraved upon it."

The same woman spoke again. "Her bracelets. She had about half a dozen of them, engraved with images of swirls and plants, words entwined by the vines. When I asked about them she told me they were love poems from the man she'd once hoped to marry. But he'd died before they could."

"Where are the bracelets now?" Kellan asked.

Chapter Twenty-Two

Meikah looked to Sarette when the vampire sighed. She had a bad feeling about the location of the bracelets. "They were buried with her." She nearly sighed as heavily as Sarette when the vampire nodded.

Kellan chuckled, draping an arm around Meikah's shoulders. "We could ask Urian to dig her up. I'm sure he's had more than enough practice."

"I'll have my people open her grave." Sarette had barely finished speaking when her people backed away. She looked at each of them. "I want two volunteers." When no one answered, she said, "Do you wish to die? Shadow's Fall want our village. Are you going to stand there instead of doing everything you can to prevent that?"

Three villagers stepped forward, shuffling their feet, their gazes fixed firmly on the ground. Their mumbles of assent barely reached Meikah who'd been about to offer to dig up the body, no matter how uncomfortable the thought made her feel. They had so little time.

"Then go dig up Naren. Why are you standing here?" Sarette demanded.

The three villagers scurried away, a fourth one joining them. Meikah watched them go, relieved she didn't need to dig up Naren. A shudder when through her at the thought.

"Are you all right?" Rafe asked.

Meikah nodded, the words she wanted to say not advisable to speak around vampires. She wouldn't make a good necromancer. The thought of digging up bodies to raise them from the dead made her feel more than a little ill. "How long is it likely to take?"

"Depends on how fast they are," Kellan said.

"I might scout the area to make sure Shadow's Fall are keeping their word." Livia turned to Rafe. "Want to join me?"

Suri, who stood beside Flint, off to the side, stepped forward. "We were going to scout the area."

Livia grinned. "The more the merrier. Might even find a couple of bandits." She glanced at Rafe, who nodded, before running towards the forest, changing form mid stride. Rafe followed her, Suri and Flint following at a slower pace.

"I will have you notified when the bracelets have been found." Sarette gave Meikah and Kellan a nod before she strode away.

Meikah watched Sarette go, surrounded by her people. "Everything is taking so long." She faced Kellan. "What will we do if we find the egg down there?" She gestured towards the cellar.

"Stay away from it."

"How are we going to return it to the dragon if we can't go near it?"

"You don't want to be marked by the scent of a dragon egg. Get closer than three feet and you could have a dragon wanting to hunt you down. And not only the mother dragon."

"That didn't answer my question."

Kellan shrugged. "I'm working on it."

"We don't have much time."

Kellan draped his arm around her shoulders. "How about we have a rest while we wait to hear from Sarette?"

"I couldn't. There's no way I could sleep with how little time we have left."

Kellan walked towards the stable, keeping his arm around Meikah's shoulders. "You won't be able to stay awake that long. Not without exhausting yourself."

He was right. She wished he wasn't. "I'll try and rest." Reaching the stable loft, she placed the lantern beside her pallet before she lay down. She was wide awake and doubted putting out the lantern would help. Unable to remain lying down for more than a few minutes, she paced the floor.

Kellan sat up. "You'll have to learn how to catch a nap when you can. There are times we hardly manage to sleep on a mission." When she continued to pace, barely glancing at him, he rose to step in front of her. "Lie down, Meikah."

"I can't. I keep thinking about all the ones who've died and the ones who might die."

"Then lie down. You need to rest while you can. You don't want to be half asleep if we have to face a dragon."

She didn't want to face a dragon at all. "How will we survive that?"

"By being very careful." Kellan grinned. "Don't worry. I'm not about to get you killed. You agreed to go somewhere with me."

A smile reluctantly formed. "That's good." She glanced down at her outfit. "I really don't want to be stuck in these clothes."

Chuckling, Kellan closed the small amount of distance that was between them, reaching for her.

A sound by the ladder had him spinning to face a villager. "Is something wrong?"

The villager shook his head.

Meikah stepped around Kellan to stand at his side. "Have the bracelets been found?"

The villager nodded. "Sarette has them. She's waiting for you at her house." The villager didn't wait for a reply, scurrying down the ladder as quickly as possible.

"What if it doesn't work?" Meikah's voice was soft, but she doubted it was soft enough that the vampires wouldn't hear. There were sure to be some nearby.

"It will." Kellan grabbed the lantern and stopped at the ladder, looking over his shoulder at her. "Ready?"

She almost told him no. Nodding, she went down the ladder, waiting for him to join her before she strode to Sarette's house. They were allowed through the door, no one stopping them, to find that the table was cleared and Sarette sat with five gold bracelets in front of her. Meikah nearly stopped walking when she saw them. She wasn't ready for this. It had only been a week since she'd learned she was a necromancer. Her steps slowed.

Kellan took hold of her hand, squeezing lightly. He placed the lantern on the table when they reached it. "Is that all of them." He nodded towards the bracelets.

Sarette shifted one of the bracelets towards him. "This one has strikes through the words. Like it was struck by lightning."

Meikah reached for one of the bracelets, stopping before she touched it. "Will anything happen to me if I touch them?"

Sarette slid the bracelet closer to Meikah. "It shouldn't. Some of my people have handled them without negative effects."

"It's saying the words that'll cause any problems," Kellan said.

Meikah examined the bracelet Sarette had pushed towards her, running her fingers over the engravings. "Which word is the first one?"

Kellan took the bracelet from her, holding it close to the lantern as he slowly turned it. He held it out to her, his fingers next to one of the words. "This one. It has a slightly different flower before it. The other words all have the same flower."

Rafe and Livia strode into the room. Rafe picked up one of the bracelets. "Are we going to test them?"

Sarette rose from the table, gathering up the bracelets left on it. "I'll have my people try them." Holding out her hand, she took the bracelets from Rafe and Meikah before striding from the room.

Meikah grabbed the lantern and followed Sarette,

her companions with her, not wanting to miss a moment of what was about to happen. They stopped in front of the open trapdoor, Sarette facing her human villagers.

"Who will read the words on the bracelets?" Sarette looked at each of the villagers gathered in front of her. None of them moved. "I need four of you." One villager stepped forward. Sarette's gaze scanned the group again. "You would leave it to only one to risk their life? Do the rest of you not care what happens to our home?" Two more shuffled forward. Sarette stared at them a moment longer before she inclined her head. "The three of you have gained a permanent place at my holding. If you wish to be transformed, come to me after this has been dealt with."

There was a murmur of thanks from the three and they stepped forward to collect bracelets, one of them taking two.

Meikah watched them walk towards the open trapdoor, wishing she could ask Rafe exactly how one became a vampire. Not that she wanted to become one. She just wanted to know. But there were no secrets to be had around here. Vampires could hear too well.

One of the villagers brought a lantern forward, handing it to the one that was trying to read from the bracelet. Once the lantern had been handed over, the villager read the words aloud.

Flames rose up around where the cottage had been, shouts running through the villagers as they leapt out of the way. Sarette's vampires converged on her, creating a protective circle around her.

"Read the words again," Kellan ordered.

Chapter Twenty-Three

Meikah clasped her hands together, wondering why Kellan didn't call rain to put out the fire. But she didn't ask. Not with the vampires listening.

The villager stumbled over the words. Nothing happened. He read them a second time, more clearly, and the flames died down.

Devin came forward and took the bracelet from the villager. "Your work is done. Give the lantern to the next one and join those who are watching."

The villager did as ordered before hurrying away, standing at the back of the group. The next villager read from the bracelet. Nothing seemed to happen. Nor for the second bracelet the villager read from.

The last villager had the bracelet that removed the sleep spell. She peered down the stairs after she'd read the words. She faced Sarette. "The darkness has gone."

Sarette turned to the crowd. "Who will enter the cellar to find out what is down there?"

When Meikah tried to step forward, Kellan drew her against his side. She wanted to protest. Surely they weren't about to let everyone else risk their lives. When she would have said something, Rafe pressed in against her other side. She glared at each of them, neither appearing to notice.

A young man came forward, taking the lantern from the woman and walking slowly down the stairs. His steps were slow, the lantern held well in front of him. "I can see an egg. It's towards the back of the room."

"Don't get too close to it," Devin said. "Stay at least three feet back. We don't want the dragon coming after our village."

"There's a table along one side with potion bottles bubbling away in different apparatuses, shelves on the opposite wall filled with bottles, ingredients and books." The young man continued his slow and steady descent, most of him now hidden from view.

Meikah wanted to go forward and check what he was doing, but Kellan and Rafe held her hands, keeping her pressed tightly between them.

"The egg is large, but not too big. It could be carried by a single person. Their arms would be full, but it would be possible. Unless it's heavier than it looks." The young man could no longer be seen. "I'm at the foot of the stairs. The egg is about four feet from me. Nothing has been damaged down here."

"Come back up," Devin ordered.

"We need to put the sleep spell back in place," Kellan said. "It'll have to be read from the base of the stairs."

"Why?" Meikah regretted the word the moment she asked it. They were meant to be saving Longview, not letting the villagers learn how little she knew.

"Yes, why would we need to do that?" Sarette asked.

Meikah felt a moment of relief to learn she wasn't the only one who didn't understand the logic of it.

"So the dragon can't track down her egg. She could be anywhere. And no one really knows the distance a dragon can track their egg," Kellan said.

Sarette inclined her head. "Read out the words." She nodded to the young man who'd come out of the cellar. "Give him the bracelet."

He took the bracelet, slowly descending the stairs once more. After a minute he could be heard reading the words before hurrying up the stairs. He held the bracelet out to Devin.

Rafe darted forward and took the bracelet before Devin could, offering it to Meikah. "If it's day when you're ready to return the egg, you won't have to wait for us vampires to wake."

She wanted to decline. That bracelet had been on the wrist of a corpse. One that had been buried. She glanced at Kellan and Livia who stood beside her. Both looked at Rafe. She started to reach for the bracelet. It wasn't the thought of touching it again that bothered her. It was looking after it until it was needed. What was she meant to do with the bracelet? Wear it?

Kellan took the bracelet before Meikah managed to, sliding it over his hand. It was a tight fit. "I'll take care of it." He grinned, meeting Meikah's gaze before turning to Sarette. "Has Naren been buried again?"

Sarette looked to Devin, who shook his head. She faced Kellan. "Why do you ask?"

"You refused to let any of your recently dead be raised by Urian, but Naren is the reason this happened. Why not have him raise her so we can order her to return the egg?" Kellan asked.

Sarette inclined her head. "That is acceptable." She turned to Devin. "Have her wrapped and slung over a horse. There's no way a cart can make it to Urian's retreat."

It didn't take long for them to saddle horses and be ready to go. It took more time to argue the need for others to come with them. Sarette had wanted to send Devin. Kellan had refused, telling her they worked alone. He also warned Sarette that they'd let Longview deal with the problem on their own if anyone followed. Sarette hadn't been happy, but had agreed.

She handed a velvet, drawstring bag to Kellan. "Give this to Urian. Tell him I'd like it back. If he wishes to return to Longview I'll fight for his right to be here."

Kellan slipped the bag into a pocket and took a lit lantern from a nearby villager. He swung into the saddle, heading towards the ravine.

Meikah followed, Livia riding behind her leading the horse Naren was slung over. She tried not to think about the body, but it was impossible to keep thoughts of it from her mind.

Rafe went on foot, flying off after a few minutes to scout the area, making sure they weren't followed. Arriving back, he became human, easily keeping up with the horses. "No one follows. I'll check again later."

"What will you do when the sun rises?" Meikah

asked. "We won't be back at Longview before then. It's probably after midnight already."

"I'll stay in Urian's cave."

Meikah glanced at the horse Livia led, continuing to find it impossible not to think about the wrapped body. "Do you think he'll help?"

"I'd be surprised if he didn't," Kellan said. "It felt like a ring in the bag Sarette gave me."

Kellan's mention of Sarette made Meikah think of her earlier questions. "Why wouldn't you let me go into the cellar?"

"This isn't our village. If they aren't willing to risk their lives to protect it, why should we be expected to?" Kellan asked.

"Is that why you didn't put out the flames with your magic?"

"No. It wouldn't have helped. They would have sprung up again."

Before Meikah could ask Rafe about becoming a vampire, he spoke.

"I'll scout the area one more time before I fly ahead and let Urian know we're coming. We don't have time to fight the zombies he'll have guarding the ravine." Rafe turned to Livia. "You remain with Meikah and Kellan. There's more noises in the forest tonight."

He was gone before Meikah could ask him what noises. She glanced around, the darkness seeming more impenetrable. What was out there? Bandits? Or something worse? She wasn't sure she wanted to know, but couldn't resist asking. "Can you hear the noises, Livia?"

"Some, but my hearing isn't as good as Rafe's."

"What is out there?" Kellan asked.

Livia shrugged. "I don't know, but it sounds like something big."

Meikah looked over her shoulder to Livia. "How big? And where is it?"

"Keep riding. If we can make it to the ravine, hopefully it'll be too big to get in there."

Livia's words didn't comfort Meikah in the least. If anything they had her peering into the darkness more frequently, trying to see what was out there. As the hours passed, she began to relax. Maybe whatever was out there wasn't interested in them. They weren't far from the entrance of the ravine when Livia shouted.

"Go. It has our scent and is coming straight for us."

Meikah leaned low over her horse, racing after Kellan, the light from the lantern he carried bobbing all over the place. "How close is it?"

"I think it's the dragon from Shadow's Fall. I can

hear wings and it's coming in above the trees," Livia said.

Meikah urged the horse to go faster. Rocks skittered and she let the horse slow, worried he'd stumble and she'd be thrown. Hearing the sound of wings behind her, she looked over her shoulder to see the dragon coming in fast, breathing flames.

"Give me your reins, Meikah," Kellan called. "Livia, time for you to do something about this."

Meikah rode beside Kellan, handing over the reins of her horse, clinging to the mane. Darkness formed around them and she was unable to see the lantern, or even the stars that had been overhead. "What is happening?"

"Quiet," Livia said. "She might not be able to see exactly where we are, but she can hear us."

Chapter Twenty-Four

The sound of wings seemed to be directly overhead. Meikah looked upwards, but could see nothing. Surely Kellan didn't plan to ride the entire way to Urian's cave in complete darkness. Or could he see through the dark Livia had settled around them? She really needed to learn how to see in the dark. Was she the only one who couldn't see in the dark in the Assassins Of The Dead at Dreyton?

Flames broke through the darkness, hitting the ground ahead of them, dying out so that the darkness pressed in around them again. Meikah clung to the horse's mane, remaining low over his neck. They were going to die. There was no way they'd survive a dragon attack. A rush of air went past her.

"That was Rafe," Livia said. "We're nearly in the ravine. Keep going."

More flames broke through the darkness. This time

off to Meikah's right. Her horse shied and she clung tightly. They better reach the ravine soon. A roar sounded above and once more flames hit the ground. They struck in front of Meikah, burning through the reins, the horse rearing and throwing her off before galloping away.

Meikah hit the ground hard, rolling to the side at the sound of more hooves. Winded, she fought for breath, unable to answer Kellan's calls. A rush of air came towards her. Before she had time to move away from it, she was cradled in familiar arms.

"Everyone keep going. I have her," Rafe called out.

She clung to Rafe, her heart racing when flames struck the ground behind them. For a moment she saw Kellan, Livia and the horse Naren was slung over, the flames between her and them. Kellan's horse reared and darkness descended before she could see what happened. "Kellan? Are you all right?"

"We're nearly in the ravine," Kellan said.

She started to protest that he hadn't answered her question. Rafe's arms tightened around her further, as he bolted around the flames that had struck directly in front of them. Fear raced through her at how close they'd been to striking Rafe. They came out of the darkness, entering the ravine. Rafe lowered her to the ground.

"You're unharmed?" Rafe's hands brushed across her arms.

"Yes. What about Kellan and Livia? I can't see anything."

"We're here." Kellan rode into the ravine, slowing the horse, flames hitting the ground behind him. "Is it safe to keep going, Rafe?"

"Urian told his zombies to let us through." Rafe pushed Meikah closer to the ravine wall.

When flames once again lit the night, Meikah saw there was a small overhang where she stood, large boulders blocking her from the flames that came towards the opening of the ravine, the vines burning away. "We can't stay here all night."

"Night is nearly over," Rafe said.

Kellan lit the lantern, dismounting to hand the reins to Rafe. "You and Livia go ahead. Meikah and I will try and convince the dragon to let us live long enough to return her egg."

Meikah didn't want to face a dragon. "Are you crazy? She'll burn us alive."

Flames came towards them and Kellan lifted a hand, a spray of water meeting them, turning instantly to steam. He glanced between Livia and Rafe. "Go. Convince Urian to raise Naren." He tossed the bag Sarette had given them to Rafe. "We'll convince the dragon that we want to help her." He placed the lantern by the boulder, at Meikah's feet.

Rafe nodded, pocketing the bag before leaping onto the back of Kellan's horse, leading the way along the ravine towards Urian's cave.

Meikah stared after Rafe and Livia for a moment before peering around the boulder at the dragon. The large creature paced back and forth, a nearby tree steadily burning. It was definitely the dark green dragon that had attacked Shadow's Fall. "How do we do this?"

"Now Naren isn't with us, she might listen." Kellan stepped into the opening. "We know what was stolen from you. We want to help." Again he was forced to send a spray of water towards the flames coming his way. "We tracked down the woman who stole your egg."

The dragon roared, stopping her pacing to face Kellan. "Then why take her from me. Give her to me now or I will burn both of you."

"Dragon's can talk?" The words escaped before Meikah could prevent them.

"Of course we can, human." The dragon said the last word like it was something far beneath her.

Meikah felt like she should apologise, but thought it best to remain silent.

"Bring me the one who stole my unborn child. Now." Steam curled from the dragon's nostrils.

"The woman is dead. We've sent her to a necromancer to be raised," Kellan said.

"What did she do with my unborn child? Why do you need to raise her?" the dragon demanded.

Meikah remained behind the boulder, peering around it, wanting to drag Kellan away from the opening of the ravine. How many more times could he draw enough moisture from the air to put out the dragon's burst of flames? It felt like there was none left, the air now dry and hot.

Kellan drew out his medallion to hold it up. "Even your race must know we work for the good of the land."

"That does not mean you will return my offspring. You might think killing me to be better for the land."

"Our king outlawed the taking of dragon eggs and the killing of dragons. The woman who stole your egg broke the law. Not a local law, but a law of the land. We will return your child to you." Kellan slipped the medallion back beneath his shirt. "But we need to help our companions with the task."

"You would expect me to trust you? My offspring is missing, you took the woman who stole my unborn child and now you wish me to let you go."

The steam rose higher, becoming thicker. "No. One of you may go and give my demands. The other is to remain with me."

"No." Meikah drew Kellan behind the boulder. "That is a terrible idea."

"My offer will not last long. Make your decision or I will destroy every village within a day's journey," the dragon warned. "None will ever dare take a child from me again."

Kellan took hold of Meikah's hands. "I'll wait with her. We'll meet you in the forest near Shadow's Fall."

"Why not near–"

Kellan interrupted her. "Shadow's Fall. Nowhere else."

She stared into his eyes that turned misty, tightening her hold on his hands. "How do we know she won't hurt you?"

"Because then she'd never have her egg returned." He let go of her hands, slipping the bracelet off to hold it out to her. "Take the lantern and go to Urian's cave." He glanced skywards. "Daylight might be coming, but that won't help much in the bottom of a ravine."

She wanted to protest. Looking past him, she saw the dragon paced back and forth, steam curling from her nostrils. How could she leave him to face the dragon alone? Her grip tightened on the bracelet.

"Meikah."

She turned to him, waiting for him to speak, expecting something serious from the tone of his voice.

Kellan grinned. "Don't get caught."

A smile reluctantly formed. "Don't you get caught either." She clasped his hand for a few seconds before letting go and grabbing the lantern. After slipping the bracelet into a pocket, she hurried away, one more glance over her shoulder. Kellan had his back to the dragon, the glow from the fire behind him making it impossible for her to see his expression. She kept going, torn between wanting to run back to him and demand the dragon let him go and running as far from the dragon as possible.

Keeping her gaze on the terrain ahead, she walked as fast as the uneven ground allowed her to go. The sun had well and truly risen by the time she reached Urian's cave, but Kellan had been right and the ravine was full of shadows and the lantern necessary. Pausing at the cave entrance, she looked around. Three horses were tied to a spindly tree, but no one was in sight.

Chapter Twenty-Five

"Hello?" Meikah's voice echoed into the cave, no reply other than her voice coming back to her. Where was everyone? She took several steps inside, not wanting to burst into the cave and upset Urian when they were in need of a favour. "Urian?" When no one answered yet again, she picked up her pace, heading to the main cave. He wasn't there. Neither was Rafe or Livia. Had something happened to them? She wandered around the area, at first thinking there was no sign of them. On the table, beside the clothbound book, was the drawstring bag. A simple ring rested on it. Picking it up, she turned the ring in her hand. There was no inscription and no stones. It was a plain gold band. Like those offered in marriage.

Placing it back on the bag, she opened the book, flicking through the pages. Cursive handwriting filled many of the pages creating something like an explorer's journal. It contained information about people, places, factions and merchant guilds.

"Where is Kellan?"

Meikah spun to face Rafe. "Where is Livia?"

"Watching Urian as he finishes raising the dead. What happened to Kellan?'

She couldn't meet Rafe's gaze. "He sent me with a message. We're to take the egg to Shadow's Fall. He and the dragon will meet us there."

"He's with the dragon? You left him with her?"

At the shock in his voice she looked at him, startled to see a flicker of flames in his eyes. "It wasn't like I wanted to." She glanced past him, seeing no one. "Where did they take Naren?"

"Further into the mountain. There's a narrow tunnel that leads to a larger cavern where Urian raises the dead." Rafe paused a moment. "I can't go outside until the sun sets. You and Livia will be on your own." Rafe glanced over his shoulder. "She'll be with us in a minute. Wait until sunset. I had expected there to be at least three of you. The forests aren't safe."

She looked past him again, but could see nothing. "We don't have time to wait." Trying not to think of the bandits that had attacked yesterday, she dredged up a reassuring smile. "We'll be fine. I'm sure Livia will tear out the throats of anyone who is foolish enough to attack us."

Livia entered the cave, grinning. "Exactly. Living or dead, it makes no difference. I'll take down any who get in the way." Behind her was Naren, staring sightlessly ahead.

Urian joined them. He started to speak, his attention caught by the open book. He crossed to the table, closing the book with a snap. "I didn't invite you to go through my things."

Meikah felt her cheeks heat, barely managing not to comment on the fact he'd told her he didn't keep up with the affairs of the world. "Sorry." So much for not upsetting the necromancer. "It's well written. Have you been to all those places?"

"No. My zombies have." He paused a moment, his voice quieter when he spoke again. "I once thought I would travel after I finished my apprenticeship with the woodworker."

"Oh." She had no idea what to say. An uncomfortable silence descended.

Urian returned the ring to the bag, tightening the drawstrings. "Tell Sarette my decision is the same. Is hers?" He held the bag out to Meikah.

Nodding, she took it from him and slipped it into

a pocket. "I will." She glanced past Livia to Naren. "Thank you for raising the dead for us."

"You could have done it if you'd chosen to," Urian said.

"It's not a choice we ever want to make." Livia turned to Rafe. "We'll see you after sunset."

Rafe nodded before facing Meikah, crossing the short distance between them in a blur. He took hold of her hand. "Don't get caught." He grinned.

The words and expression, so close to Kellan's, made her feel guilty for needing to leave both of them behind. "I'll meet you in the forest near Shadow's Fall."

"I'll find you." Rafe's grip momentarily tightened before he let go of her hand and stepped back.

Livia strode towards the exit, glancing over her shoulder to speak to Naren. "Follow me. Stay close."

Meikah followed behind Naren, avoiding getting too close. She waited until they were outside before she spoke to Livia. "I thought Urian might not be able to raise Naren since she isn't exactly recently dead."

Livia swung into the saddle of her horse, ordering Naren to ride the horse she'd been slung over earlier. "He did the raising, but drew on my power to raise an older corpse."

Meikah mounted Kellan's horse, following Livia

and Naren into the ravine. "Necromancers can do that?"

Livia looked over her shoulder at Meikah. "Yeah, but don't ever let a necromancer you don't trust use your power unless you have someone there to look out for you. It can be dangerous."

"That's why none of you answered me when I first arrived at the cave?"

Livia nodded, facing forward. "Rafe waited until Urian had finished using my power before he went to you."

They fell silent until they reached the end of the ravine. The tree no longer burned, ash scattered around the base, the trunk charred. Meikah halted the horse. "He's gone." She hadn't expected that. "Do you think-" She couldn't finish her question.

Livia stopped not far from Meikah. "Kellan would have convinced the dragon to go with him so we didn't risk her wanting to attack Naren." She smiled reassuringly. "He'll be fine. He knows what he's doing."

She really hoped he did. Taking a deep breath, she dragged her gaze from the burnt tree. "Let's collect the egg and give it to the dragon so we can get Kellan back." When Livia nodded, she continued towards Longview.

Things didn't go as planned in Longview and they spent ages arguing with the humans Sarette had left in charge. None of them wanted to do anything until Sarette woke. Meikah's hand went to the hilt of her sword, tempted to draw it. "We don't have time for this. Do you want the attacks to resume?" She doubted they'd care what happened to Kellan if they failed to give the egg to the dragon in a reasonable amount of time.

"You need to wait for Sarette to wake," the villager repeated.

Taking another deep breath didn't help. Meikah held up the gold bracelet Kellan had given her. "Sarette would not have allowed me to keep this if she didn't want me to use it." She felt power course through her and tried to control it.

The villager took several steps back. "You need to-"

"No." Meikah stalked towards him. "I will not wait for Sarette." She could feel her power crackle around her and saw the lightning in her eyes reflected back at her from the eyes of the villager. "Get out of my way." When the villager stepped to the side, she strode towards the trapdoor he'd tried to block. She wasn't about to leave Kellan with the dragon any longer than necessary.

Livia strode beside Meikah, Naren continuing to follow her. "We can't kill the villagers."

"I don't plan to."

Livia chuckled. "Not even accidentally."

"The dragon didn't sound patient." She stopped at the trapdoor, looking down the stairs at the darkness.

"Dragons never are. Not when it comes to their eggs or their territory." Livia looked from the darkness to Meikah. "Did you want me to read the bracelet?"

Meikah held it up, silently reading the words before speaking them aloud. The darkness drew in on itself, becoming nothing, the egg visible. She remained at the top of the stairs, not wanting to get any closer to the egg than necessary. She didn't want any dragons hunting her. She had more than enough problems without adding that to the list.

Livia took a step into the cellar. "I wonder if Sarette will let us keep the bracelet. That spell could come in handy."

Suri walked towards them. "She'll claim ownership of it once all this is over." Suri stopped beside Meikah. "Do you need a hand with anything?"

Meikah turned to Livia, not sure if Suri could be trusted. She might be a member of the Assassins Of

The Dead, but who knew exactly what that meant. She certainly didn't.

Livia nodded. "That'd be good. We'll step out of the way and I'll send Naren down to pick up the egg. You can help us guard her and the egg. With all this fighting going on there are probably more bandits than usual in the area. Somehow they always seem to know when an area is vulnerable."

Chapter Twenty-Six

Meikah stepped back from the trapdoor, noticing that a few villagers watched them from the shadows created by burnt out buildings. "Will Naren be able to ride a horse to Shadow's Fall?"

Livia finished backing away from the cellar opening. "I have no idea how she'd get on a horse while carrying an egg and I certainly don't plan on getting that close to it."

"She can walk," Suri said. "Better taking longer to return the egg than to rush these things and not make it there at all."

Meikah wanted to argue with Suri that neither suggestion suited her. Kellan had to remain with the dragon until they could rescue him. And the dragon wouldn't wait indefinitely. She could think of no other way to get the egg to the dragon. Not without causing other problems. "We'll walk."

Livia turned to Naren. "Collect the dragon egg that's in the cellar and bring it up here. Make sure you remain four feet away from each of us."

Meikah watched as Naren did as she'd been told, standing patiently once she had the egg out of the cellar. The shell of the egg caught a shaft of sunlight, a ripple of light shimmering across the top of it. "What happened?"

"The egg lives."

"We have to exchange it for Kellan before we risk that changing." Meikah continued to watch the egg, the ripple of light crossing the surface another two times.

"I'll collect the horses." Suri took one more look at the dragon's egg before she strode off to saddle horses and ready saddlebags.

Meikah waited until Suri was out of hearing range. "Can we trust her?"

Livia nodded. "She's an Assassin Of The Dead. They don't last long in the faction if they're corrupt."

"I know so little."

Livia grinned. "You'll pick it up as we go along."

"I hope so." A sound had Meikah spinning in that direction.

Suri led three horses, all of them appearing quiet

and well behaved. "A couple of the villagers were already saddling them."

Livia took the reins of one of the horses, swinging into the saddle. "Time to rescue Kellan."

Meikah slipped the bracelet back into her pocket, not knowing what else to do with it. She wasn't about to leave it with one of the villagers. "It's going to be a slow trip." She glanced at Naren before swinging into the saddle.

"Then we better get going." Livia turned to Naren. "Follow me without getting closer than four feet. You must maintain that distance at all times." Livia urged the horse to take a couple of steps towards Naren. The woman took a couple of steps back. Livia grinned. "Looks like this is going to work."

Meikah rode ahead, Suri dropping behind. It was late afternoon. Nearly another sunset gone. Meikah kept glancing skywards. They were running out of time to get everything done. Larkin hadn't seemed like the type to give them extra time. Not that she blamed him. His village was being destroyed by a dragon.

They were over halfway to Shadow's Fall when six bandits came towards them, mounted on horses. The one in the middle grinned, turning to the men on either side of him. "Now that ain't something you see all the time. A dragon egg away from its mamma."

The shortest bandit returned the other one's grin, drawing a dagger. "Reckon we should relieve them of their burden. Wouldn't want them to be caught with something illegal."

Livia raised her hands, light seemed to fade from the day around her, the effect stretching out for several feet around her. "Naren remain where you are. Meikah, read the sleep spell over her."

One of the bandits leapt from his horse, a dagger in each hand as he threw himself towards Meikah. She nearly dropped the bracelet, about to draw her sword when Livia leapt in front, changing forms as she landed on the bandit, slamming him into the dirt, snarling. Trying to concentrate, Meikah faced Naren, the sound of fighting around her as she read out the words of the spell.

Suri tossed one of the bandits into the darkness the moment it formed, the other bandits backing away when their companion disappeared into the sleep spell. "Who's next?" Suri strode towards another bandit.

Meikah started to draw her sword, her hand remaining on the hilt when the bandits turned as one and ran for their horses, riding away. "What about the one left behind? The moment the spell is ended, he'll wake up."

Suri moved closer to the spell, Livia stalking around to the other side. Suri nodded to Meikah. "Bring it down."

Staying on her horse, Meikah read the words, slipping the bracelet back into her pocket to reach for her sword. The bandit looked at each of them, shaking his head in confusion. When Livia roared, sharp teeth visible, he bolted for his horse. He headed in the same direction his companions had taken.

Suri laughed, returning her battleaxe to her back. "As disappointing as that fight was, his expression was rather enjoyable." She strode to her horse and swung into the saddle, glancing skywards. "Not much light left in the day now. Better get moving before something else comes out of the forest."

Meikah wasn't about to argue. Time was running out.

Livia called a halt in a clearing, well after dark. Suri had taken a lantern from the saddlebags on her horse, lighting it and giving it to Meikah, when night had fallen.

"We aren't far from Kellan and the dragon. Naren, stay where you are." Livia moved further away from the zombie before turning to Meikah. "Read out the sleep spell. I want to make certain the dragon will exchange the egg for Kellan and the safety of the villages before we give it to her."

Meikah remained on her horse, reading out the spell again, watching as the darkness spread out to engulf Naren and the egg. "How far are we from Kellan?"

"Ten minutes or so. The dragon could probably tell her egg was getting closer. I'm not sure what she'll think now she can no longer sense it," Livia said.

Fear raced through Meikah. "Lead the way to Kellan." The dragon better not hurt him. She followed Livia, who cantered through the forest, none of them able to go any faster with how close the trees grew. Seeing Kellan, leaning against a tree near the dragon, she leapt from the horse, leaving the lantern on the ground to throw her arms around him. "You're safe."

A rumble came from the dragon. "Not for much longer if you don't return my unborn child. What did you do? I can no longer sense where my child is." Steam rose from the dragon's nostrils and a growling rumble began as she came closer to Meikah and Kellan.

A bat flew down to land next to Meikah, becoming human. "Do I get such an enthusiastic greeting?"

Meikah let go of Kellan to wrap her arms around Rafe. "You're safe too. I was worried about both of you." She never wanted to leave either of them behind again. What if something had happened to one of them?

The dragon's rumble became a roar. "You can worry about every village around here if you do not return my offspring immediately."

Livia faced the dragon, remaining at a distance. "We have your egg. It's safe. We want your word you won't retaliate against anyone other than the woman who arranged for your egg to be taken. And that you won't harm any of us."

"If my offspring is returned to me unharmed you have my word you are safe and I will not take my revenge on any other than the one who caused my offspring to be kidnapped." Steam continued to rise from the dragon's nostrils. "If I find the smallest of cracks in the egg I will make each of you pay seven fold."

Livia gave a single nod. "This way."

Meikah collected the lantern, mounted her horse and held out a hand to Kellan who swung up behind her. She followed Livia and Suri, Rafe running at her side. It didn't take long to reach the clearing, stopping at the opposite side of where the dragon egg was hidden by the sleep spell.

"Where is my offspring?" the dragon demanded.

Once Kellan was off the horse, Meikah dismounted. "The egg is here." She strode towards the darkness, placing the lantern on the ground next to her before taking out the bracelet. She read the words, almost knowing them off by heart after the amount of times she'd spoken them. But knowing the words wouldn't help her use the spell without the bracelet it had been bound to. The darkness drew in on itself and Naren rose to her feet, picking up the egg. Meikah faced the dragon, opening her mouth to tell her the egg was all hers as she stepped away from it. She didn't have the chance to speak.

A larger dragon flew into the clearing, roaring, flames aimed at the first dragon, his charcoal coloured scales making it difficult to see him. "My territory." He roared again, claws outstretched as he attacked the dragon. "No one invades my territory."

The first dragon dodged, awkwardly taking to the sky.

With another roar, the second dragon flew towards the egg. "Not taking over my territory." Flames came towards the egg and Naren.

Chapter Twenty-Seven

Meikah automatically dived towards the egg, worried the deal they'd made with the dragon would be broken. Tackling Naren to the ground, she wrapped her arms around the egg, rolling away, flames rushing above them. Would the dragon consider the deal unmet if the egg was destroyed in this battle?

Naren rose jerkily to her feet, her arms stretched towards Meikah and the egg. Before Naren could take a step towards them, flames engulfed her. The zombie screamed, raising her hands to cover her head. It didn't help.

Meikah looked away. Obviously sentient zombies felt pain, unlike other zombies. Staggering to her feet, she looked around, spotting the two dragons in combat. The smaller one wasn't doing well.

"Meikah, drop the egg and I'll carry you from here." Rafe stood three feet from her.

She shook her head. "I can't." She took several steps backwards, trying to figure out what to do. "We promised to return the egg unharmed." And running wouldn't help. The scent of the egg would cling to her forever. Unless the dragon took it from her.

"We've already returned it unharmed," Rafe said.

Meikah shook her head again, glancing around the clearing. Kellan, Livia and Suri were at various locations around the edge, looking between her and the fighting dragons, dragon flames casting a flickering light over the area. She took a step backwards, not knowing what to do.

The first dragon plummeted to the ground, catching herself at the last second, skimming across the ground before landing heavily, collapsing. She struggled to rise.

The other dragon landed in front of her, stalking towards her. "I wake from a lengthy sleep to find you've tried to take my territory."

"I was searching for my unborn child. It was never a bid for your territory." The first dragon staggered, unsuccessfully trying to retreat.

"Lies." The second dragon roared, opening his mouth to throw flames at the first dragon.

Meikah's jaw dropped, a crazy plan forming in her mind as the first dragon managed to avoid the flames. Placing the egg carefully on the ground, she ran towards the second dragon, raising the bracelet to read the words by the light of dragon fire, ignoring Kellan and Rafe's demands to retreat.

The spell formed in front of her, settling over the second dragon, catching the wing of the first dragon in its circle. The flames died instantly, darkness descending, the lantern too far from her to help. Meikah froze, worried she might stumble into the spell. "I can't see."

Flames shot past Meikah, igniting a patch of tall grass. "I cannot draw my wing from the spell." The dragon lay on her side, her wing at an awkward angle.

Meikah slowly walked towards her. "I can try and pull your wing from the spell, but if I lift the spell, the other dragon will wake."

"Leave the spell intact. He would kill my unborn child." The dragon struggled ineffectually. "Sleep drags at me, the spell slowing my ability to heal."

Meikah slid the bracelet onto her wrist so she didn't lose it, trying not to think about the previous owner. She tugged at the wing. It didn't move. She tried again, leaning back to use her weight. Nothing happened. "You're too heavy. I can't-"

Rafe reached Meikah's side in a blur. "I can. Move

out of the way." He tugged the wing from the spell, standing between Meikah and the dragon.

The dragon rose unsteadily to her feet, lowering her head to face Rafe. "Out of the way, vampire. Do you think I would harm the one who risked herself for my unborn child?"

Meikah pushed Rafe to the side, coming closer to the dragon. "Can you take the scent of your egg from me?"

"I will do better than that." The dragon rose above her, breathing heavily.

Meikah felt warmth wash over her. "I don't need anything else." All she wanted was for them to be safe. For the dragon to abide by the deal she'd made earlier.

"Hold out your right hand, palm down."

Meeting the dragon's gaze, Meikah did as she was told. The warmth turned to a heat in her hand. Before she could draw it back, the dragon placed her paw on top of her hand, the heat increasing.

"I owe you the life of my unborn child. Letha calls you protector of dragons. That all dragons will know you mean them no harm you shall be marked by my touch."

"Letha, this isn't-" Meikah broke off at the rush of heat through her veins. For a split second it felt like her entire body was on fire, the heat beginning to decrease the moment it had flared.

"It is necessary." Letha looked past her. "It will allow you to face him safely when you undo the spell." Letha drew back her paw.

Meikah stared at her hand. Warmth settled into her veins, a mark flaring on the back of her hand before fading into her skin. The silhouette of a dragon in flight. Her mouth gaped and she was unable to speak. The dragon touched were a myth from ancient times. Warriors that protected dragons against those who would take their hoard from them. No one believed they'd ever existed. A tale the dragons had created to make warriors think twice about coming after them. She couldn't drag her gaze from the back of her hand even though the mark was no longer visible.

"I will take my unborn child home and return with an offering for the one whose territory I had to invade. You will make peace for me."

Before Meikah could argue, Letha crossed the clearing to her egg, picking it up to cradle it close. Sending one more burst of flames at the corpse of Naren, she took to the sky, her flight awkward and slow.

Rafe stepped closer to Meikah, taking her hand. "This is an honour." He turned her hand to stare at the back of it, no sign of the mark visible. As Kellan, Livia and Suri came close, he formed a fireball in his other hand and held it close to Meikah's hand.

She stared at the mark that darkened on her skin. "I don't deserve this. I was trying to save us."

Rafe let the fireball die out, the mark fading on Meikah's hand. "You do deserve it. Would you ever kill a dragon?"

She glanced towards the sleep spell. "It's illegal."

Kellan grinned. "That wouldn't have stopped you if you'd really wanted to kill one." He took her hand from Rafe's, examining the skin in the dying light of the grass fire.

Suri touched the back of Meikah's hand. "Return to King's Peak with me. We need you here in the Arcton Mountains. We have no one who can negotiate with dragons."

Rafe and Kellan stepped in close to Meikah, both speaking at the same time. "She belongs in Dreyton," Kellan said.

"Dreyton is her home," Rafe stated.

"She could save hundreds of lives," Suri said.

Kellan draped an arm around Meikah's shoulders. "She already has."

"Anyone can work in Dreyton. No one else is protected from dragons," Suri argued.

Livia stepped between Meikah and Suri so the woman had to step back. "You've made your offer. If she wants to take you up on it, she will. Leave her alone."

Meikah felt guilty for wanting to refuse. Suri was right. Anyone could work in Dreyton. She opened her mouth to speak. Before she could, Rafe scooped her up and took her from the clearing, her unspoken words becoming a gasp. "Put me down."

Rafe came to a stop, lowering Meikah to the ground. "Don't do something you'd regret."

She tried to see his expression, but it was dark away from the grass fire. "You don't-"

"I heard your sigh. It was soft, but loud enough for me. I felt your shoulders lower where they rested against my arm and I could almost feel you trying to force yourself to say yes. You're not a templar. There's no need for you to live by their code of protect and serve."

She opened her mouth to argue with him, closing it when she realised he was right.

Rafe laughed softly. "Are you going to say no now?"

"Take me back, Rafe."

He scooped her up in his arms, remaining still. "Are you?"

Chapter Twenty-Eight

Meikah resisted the wry smile that wanted to escape, knowing Rafe would be able to see it in the dark. "I should be annoyed at you for dragging me away like that." But it had given her time to think. It was difficult breaking the habit of years of living by the code of protect and serve. "Take me back."

"You've made a decision."

"Yes."

"I hope it's the right one."

Clinging to Rafe, she hoped it was too. They reached the clearing to find the fire nearly out and Suri arguing with Kellan and Livia. Meikah strode towards them the moment Rafe let her go. "I'm returning to Dreyton."

Suri stopped mid sentence. "But you can–"

"Dreyton is my home. I can't desert my home." Thoughts of Magan and the army she'd raised came to mind followed by the many people she cared about. "My friends and family need me."

Suri stared at her a moment longer before she nodded. "I understand. But if we were desperately in need of your help, would you come?"

Kellan and Livia stood on one side of Meikah, Rafe on the other. Kellan slung an arm around Livia and Meikah's shoulders, grinning. "That wouldn't happen to be every other day of the week, would it?"

Suri smiled wryly. "As much as I'd like to call on her help that often, I meant what I said. It would be in an emergency."

Meikah nodded, prevented from saying anything by the return of Letha. She stepped away from her friends and past Suri, who turned to face the dragon. "Your unborn child is safely in your nest?"

Letha dipped her head before tossing a large leather bag onto the ground in front of Meikah. "For the dragon of this territory. When you rouse him, hold up your right hand, palm towards you. Tell him you're dragon touched before he has the chance to do anything, even rise from the ground. He will accord you all courtesies." Letha took to the sky.

Meikah stared after the dragon, who had rapidly disappeared into the darkness of the night. She was really going to have to work on being able to see in the dark. That would be handier than being able to negotiate with dragons since there were none in Dreyton.

Suri picked up the bag and looked inside, her mouth gaping momentarily. "There's a fortune in here." She held it out to Meikah.

Peering in the bag, Meikah saw a mixture of jewels and gold, the last of the firelight catching on the shiny surfaces. "No wonder people once went after dragons, before the King outlawed it." She took the bag from Suri, nearly dropping it when she found it was heavier than she'd expected.

Livia brought the lantern over to Meikah before the fire died out. "What do we do now?"

Meikah looked at each of her companions. "I'll face him. The rest of you leave the clearing." It took her nearly half an hour to convince Kellan, Rafe and Livia that she had to do it alone. That she'd be safer without them at her side. It was Suri who eventually convinced them. Meikah placed the lantern at her feet and the bag of treasure at the edge of the sleep spell.

Slipping the bracelet off her wrist, she once more tried not to think about who'd previously worn it. It was a little difficult not to with the charred remains of Naren not far from her. Taking a deep breath, she read out the words, returning the bracelet to her wrist as the darkness drew in on itself. Meikah raised her hand, calling out, "I am dragon touched."

The dragon staggered to his feet, stretching his wings as he faced her. "There are none around here who have been touched by dragons."

She continued to hold up her hand. "I am dragon touched." When a rush of warm air washed over her from the dragon, she held herself still when she would have preferred to retreat.

"Dragon touched." The dragon stared at her silently for a moment. "Where is the one who invaded my territory?"

Meikah lowered her hand, gesturing towards the bag sitting between them. "It was a misunderstanding. She was hunting down the one who stole her unborn child. She sends this peace offering for any offence she may have caused."

"Tell me everything." The dragon settled on the ground, folding his wings in close.

"Everything?" That would take hours. Surely he didn't expect her to tell him every little detail.

The dragon inclined his head. "Everything. No matter how many hours it might take to satisfy my curiosity." He looked past Meikah. "Start with the one who wants to approach."

Meikah turned to see Rafe stood a few feet into the

clearing, holding a timber stool and a lantern. "He's a friend."

Rafe took several steps towards them. "I know dragons enjoy a long tale. You have made yourself comfortable in preparation. I've brought a stool to allow Meikah to do the same."

The dragon gestured Rafe forward.

Meikah stared at Rafe, closing her mouth when she realised it was open. Dragons enjoyed a long tale? How long? She had to let Shadow's Fall know that the problem had been solved, not spend hours talking to a dragon.

Rafe placed the stool beside her. "I borrowed this from Larkin. He expects me to return with the information he's waiting for. The rest will remain nearby."

"Thank you." Meikah sat on the stool, relieved her friends were taking care of their mission. She looked up at the dragon trying to figure out where she should start the story. In the end, she started with Flint arriving in Dreyton, asking for help.

It took hours to answer the dragon's many questions and it was late morning before he gathered the bag of treasure and flew away. She staggered when she rose from the stool, having sat for too long. Seeing Kellan walk towards her, she picked up the stool and lantern and met him partway. "Where is everyone?"

Kellan took the stool from her and beckoned two humans forward, handing the stool to one of them and taking the reins of their horses from the other human. "Thank Larkin for the use of the stool."

The humans nodded. They returned to the forest without a word, their eyes round as they glanced over their shoulders at Meikah.

Their glances made Meikah uncomfortable. She hadn't done anything to deserve them. It had been an accident. All she'd wanted was to protect her friends.

Kellan took Meikah's hand. "Can you ride or are you likely to fall asleep?"

"I can ride." She glanced around. "Where is everyone?"

Kellan took the lantern and helped her onto the horse. "Suri negotiated the use of some of the sentient zombies to help rebuild Longview and took them back with her. Livia returned to Longview with Rafe and should be back shortly. I told her to bring food otherwise she'd probably already be here." He mounted his horse, grinning. "I don't know about you, but I'm starving."

She yawned. "I'd rather sleep."

"Maybe you should have asked the dragon to give

you a lift to Longview." Kellan grinned. "It would have given him the chance to ask you more questions."

Meikah slowly shook her head. "I didn't know dragons were so curious."

Kellan chuckled. "Worse than the gossips of Dreyton."

Chapter Twenty-Nine

Meikah smiled, too tired to say anything. She was nearly falling off her horse by the time Livia found them, turning human and joining Meikah on her horse. Meikah was too tired to argue Livia's comment that she looked like she was about to fall off her horse, taking some of the food Livia had brought back with her.

Meikah barely remembered the rest of the journey to Longview or climbing up the ladder to the stable loft. She slept till late afternoon, waking in time to say goodbye to Flint and Suri who needed to return to King's Peak.

Flint gave Kellan a silk scarf for the Duchess, telling him he thought they might prefer not to extend their journey by having to travel to King's Peak. It was wrapped in soft cotton and stored in a carved timber box. When Kellan opened it to examine the fine fabric, Meikah wasn't surprised that King's Peak were famous for their scarves. She couldn't resist touching the fabric. It was a pale pearl blue, a colour she'd never seen before in a fabric.

Kellan grinned. "The Duchess is going to love this. I wonder what she'll send us after next."

Meikah slowly shook her head. "I'm hoping there won't be another journey like this."

Kellan's grin remained in place. "Where's your sense of adventure?"

"I think I left it at home." Or it had been lost some time during her rather lengthy conversation with the dragon.

"Next time bring it with you," Livia said. "Makes things a lot more interesting." She grinned with a glance at Kellan. "Or so I've been told."

Once Suri and Flint had left, Meikah, Kellan and Livia were invited to a meal with the human villagers while they waited for the sun to set. At sunset they returned to the loft to let Rafe out of the coffin, the four of them following Devin who led them to where Sarette sat at her table, two goblets filled to the brim. She offered one to Rafe, after taking a sip from it.

Meikah handed over the velvet drawstring bag. "Urian asked me to tell you that his decision is the same. Is yours?"

Sarette tipped the ring into her hand, staring at it for a moment. "I thought he might have changed his mind." She looked to Rafe. "Particularly after meeting you. It's obvious a vampire can be a necromancer." Her gaze returned to the ring and after staring at it for a few seconds longer, she returned it to the drawstring bag, nodding towards the bracelet Meikah wore. "I believe that belongs to Longview."

Meikah slipped it off, handing it over, glad she no longer had to worry about losing it.

"We'll leave in the morning," Kellan said.

"Are you the one who is in charge of this group?" Sarette asked.

Kellan nodded.

Sarette gestured one of her villagers forward, nodding towards Kellan. The villager handed over a small, leather drawstring pouch, stepping back once the task was completed.

Kellan tucked the pouch away. "Thank you."

Sarette inclined her head. "If you have need of any supplies for your journey home, let Devin know and he'll see that they are found."

"We have enough for our journey," Livia said.

"Then safe travels," Sarette said.

The four of them started for the exit.

"Rafe."

Rafe turned at Sarette's call, crossing to her side in a blur when she gestured him to her.

Meikah watched as he lowered his head, nodding to whatever Sarette had to say. He nodded a second time before he returned to her side in a blur. She wanted to ask him what Sarette had said, but the vampire would hear her question. She'd ask him when they were back in Dreyton.

She clambered up the ladder into the stable loft, expecting her friends to join her. When several minutes passed and they didn't come up the ladder, she looked through the trapdoor. "Is something wrong?"

Livia was first up the ladder, grinning at her. "No."

Kellan was last, holding out the leather, drawstring pouch. "For you, minus the coins we need to give Danton."

Meikah frowned, not taking the pouch. "What do you mean? Why is it for me?"

"It's the money we were paid for helping Flint and Suri. Half of what they were paid," Kellan said.

"But–" She frowned, trying to make sense of what Kellan was telling her. "It can't be mine."

He grinned. "I spoke to Rafe and Livia. They agreed you can have it."

Her eyes narrowed at his grin. "Why?" She didn't bother keeping the suspicion from her voice.

Livia chuckled. "For battle gear. I'd hate to think you might die in that outfit." She nodded towards the clothes Meikah wore.

"I can't take that. We all earned it."

Rafe took the pouch from Kellan, placing it in Meikah's hand. "You were the one who earned it by saving the egg. We thought you'd die when you did that."

"If you plan to keep taking crazy risks, you better get yourself measured up for battle gear," Livia said.

"It didn't seem crazy at the time." She stared at the pouch in her hand. Well, it had, but not as crazy as it had seemed after she'd thought about it some more.

"It never does." Kellan's grin widened. "Talking of crazy, we need to work on getting you thrown out of the Dark Blade Academy. This trip slowed that plan down a bit."

Meikah backed away. "Nothing crazy. Not like your last plan."

"What was wrong with my last plan? You wait and see, the gossips will still be talking about the 'flag' and the parade," Kellan said. "But don't worry, I'll come up with something better for getting you thrown out of the academy. You'll love it."

"Better?" The word sounded like a squeak. "Don't worry?" Her voice was higher pitched than usual. She had a feeling she should start worrying. Her gaze was drawn to the pouch she held. Battle gear might be a very good idea if she continued to follow Kellan and his crazy plans.

Livia laughed, draping an arm around Meikah's shoulders. "Put your money away and help with the planning. That way you might be happier with what he drags you into."

The rest of the evening was spent arguing Kellan's many ideas, talking over what they planned to do when they returned home and wondering what had been happening in Dreyton while they were gone. All of them except Rafe went to sleep around midnight. He remained awake, keeping watch until it was time for his coffin to be loaded on the wagon and for him to lie inside, the lid chained shut for the journey home.

Chapter Thirty

Meikah began to think it would be an uneventful journey as they travelled harmlessly through the Arcton Mountains. A few times she thought she caught sight of a dragon flying overhead. Each time there was nothing above when she looked. When the sun set, Rafe joined Meikah on the seat, driving since he saw the best in the dark.

"What did Sarette say to you?"

Rafe was silent for a moment. "It's something I need to think about."

"Did she want you to stay in Longview?"

Rafe rested his hand on hers for a moment. "No. Nothing like that."

"Is there a problem?" She really needed to learn how to see in the dark. It was frustrating being the only one who couldn't.

"You don't need to-" Rafe broke off. "Light." The

lanterns lit up, showing bandits coming towards them. Rafe drew the wagon to a stop.

Meikah leapt to the ground, shielding her eyes when one of the bandits threw something on the ground that caused a flare of light. She drew her sword, lightning crawling along the blade.

"Necromancer!" the bandit closest to Meikah cursed.

She met his blade, drawing her dagger as well. "Better than being a bandit." She drove him back, anger at his words fuelling her attacks. He stumbled, falling to land on his back, his sword clattering across the ground.

"Meikah!"

She spun at Kellan's cry, seeing another bandit coming for her, ducking the swing of his greatsword. The bandit lying at her feet knocked her sword from her hand when she stumbled back and it was her that ended up on the ground, Kellan calling her name again. Lightning flared across her right hand as she automatically raised it when the greatsword swung towards her.

The mark on the back of her hand flared along with the lightning. It struck out at the bandit, a lacey pattern of lightning in the form of a winged creature, knocking him backwards. Meikah remained on the ground, staring at the bandit who backed away, stumbling over his friend who lay on the ground.

Rafe stood over Meikah, holding out his hand, helping her to her feet when she took it. "Are you unharmed?" He ran his hands down her arms. "I smell no blood on you."

She shook her head, unable to speak. Around them was silence. Raising her right hand, she stared at the unmarked skin. Both the mark and lightning had faded. "How… what…" She shook her head again.

Kellan and Livia crowded around her, both reaching for her.

She took a step backwards. "What happened?"

Rafe's gaze was drawn to Meikah's hand. "I've never heard a single tale about a dragon touched who was a necromancer. Or a sorcerer. They're usually warriors."

Kellan took her hand, running his thumb over the back of it. "That was amazing. I've never seen anything like it before."

She drew her hand from his light grip, shaking her head. As if she didn't have enough problems. "What happened to the bandits?"

Livia grinned. "You scared them. I don't think they knew what to make of you. One called you a demon before running. They even left behind their fallen friends."

Kellan hoisted the bandit Meikah had struck with her lightning onto his shoulder. "We'll take them to Dreyton. The law can deal with them."

Once the four bandits were on the back of the wagon and secured with rope, they continued their journey. Most of the lanterns were off, Meikah having protested when they'd wanted to put all of them out. She sat beside Rafe again, staring at her hand that rested in her lap.

Rafe draped an arm around her shoulders. "We'll stand by you. No matter what it means." He glanced at her hand.

She leaned against his shoulder. "Do you think Letha knows what it means?" Not that she wanted to return to the Arcton Mountains. In the distance she could see the lights of Dreyton. They were almost home. She sat up straight.

"I'll go with you if you want to find her and ask," Rafe said.

Kellan leaned forward. "I'll go with you too."

Livia, who'd been lying in the coffin, clambered out. "You're not leaving me behind." She put the lid back into place so she could sit on top of the coffin.

Meikah smiled, looking at each of her friends.

"Thanks. But I don't think I'm up to another trip to the Arcton Mountains any time soon." She had other things to figure out first. Like learning how to see in the dark.

The dirt road they travelled across became cobblestones as they entered Dreyton. It was early in the night. They'd begun their journey home earlier than they'd started out on their mission to Longview. People wandered along the footpath, some stopping to watch them drive past. They were a block from Fable when they saw a group gathered on the footpath.

Some of those gathered carried boards with words painted on them, chanting over and over again, "The dead should remain dead. The dead should remain dead." Occasionally one of them broke from the chant, saying, "All vampires must be staked. We're not cattle for them to feed on."

A shiver ran through Meikah when she saw the sharp, wooden stakes some of them held. Some of those gathered held out pamphlets and a few people stopped to talk to them. She slipped an arm around Rafe. "They're the ones who should be staked. They're as bad as those who think all necromancers are the same."

"Who do they think they are?" Livia demanded.

Rafe's words were soft. "The Society Against Vampires." He was silent a moment. "Vampires always die when they arrive in a town."

One of the chanters stepped to the edge of the footpath as the wagon drove past, pointing at them. "There's one now. Come to prey on your families. Come to turn your children into blood drinking monsters."

Livia's hand went to the hilt of her sword. "I'll show them monsters." She started to rise from the coffin.

Kellan placed a hand on her shoulder. "They haven't done anything other than talk."

Livia glared at the Society Against Vampires. "The moment they do, I'm going after them."

Meikah turned her head so she could watch them too, taking hold of Rafe's hand, his other one holding the reins. She agreed with Livia. The moment they did something she was going after them. No one was going to harm Rafe. Not while she was alive. Her lips curved into a smile. Which was a very long time since necromancers couldn't die.

Free Ebook

Subscribe to Avril's newsletter and receive a free ebook. This ebook is exclusive to those on her mailing list. To find out more about this offer visit: www.avrilsabine.com/free-ebook

*

We value your privacy and will not sell, rent, exchange or loan your email address to third parties. Your information is confidential and you are under no obligation to remain on the mailing list and can unsubscribe at any time.

Acknowledgements

Many thanks, as always, to my usual crew. I couldn't manage without you.

To The Reader

If you enjoyed this book, why not consider leaving a review to help other readers discover it too? Reader engagement is one of the few ways that lets an author know readers want more books in a particular series or genre. So leave a review and tell friends, not only about this book but also about other ones you've enjoyed, so you can continue to enjoy books by your favourite authors for years to come.

Dreams are meant to be lived,

Avril.

About The Author

Avril is an Australian author who lives with her family on acreage in South East Queensland. She writes mostly young adult and children's speculative fiction, but has been known to dabble in other genres. You can find more information about her at www.avrilsabine.com where you can also subscribe to her newsletter to be kept informed about new releases, current projects, blog posts and exclusive news.

Titles By Avril Sabine

Stories about strong characters and characters who discover their strengths.

SERIES

Assassins Of The Dead- Young Adult Fantasy/ Paranormal

Book 1: Dark Blade

Book 2: Dragon Touched

Book 3: Society Against Vampires

Book 4: King's Request

Book 5: Duke's Courier

Dragon Blood- Young Adult Urban Fantasy (with elements of romance)

(5 book series)

Book 1: Pliethin

Book 2: Wyvern

Book 3: Surety

Book 4: Knight

Book 5: Mage

Dragon Mage- Young Adult Urban Fantasy (with elements of romance)

(Series two of Dragon Blood series)

Book 1: Promise

Book 2: Pact

Dragon Blood Chronicles- Young Adult Urban Fantasy (with elements of romance)

(Companion stand alone series to Dragon Blood)

Book 1: Oath

Book 2: Betrayed

Guardians Of The Round Table- Young Adult Fantasy LitRPG

(Co-written with Storm and Rhys Petersen)

Book 1: Dexterity Fail

Book 2: Goblin Boots

Book 3: Singed Feathers

Book 4: Frog Mage

Book 5: Crystal Mine

Book 6: Cursed Harp

Rosie's Rangers- Young Adult Western Steampunk

(6 book series)

Book 1: Justice

Book 2: Vengeance

Book 3: Treachery

Book 4: Accused

Book 5: Wanted

Book 6: Corruption

Mark Of Kings- Children's Fantasy

(Upper middle grade/preteen)

(4 book series)

Book 1: The Arena

Book 2: The Island

Book 3: The Assassin

Book 4: The King

STAND ALONE SERIES

Demon Hunters- Young Adult Urban Fantasy/ Horror (with elements of romance)

Book 1: Blood Sacrifice

Book 2: Retribution

Book 3: Tainted

Book 4: Premonition

Book 5: Cursed

Book 6: Feud

Book 7: Extrication

Plea Of The Damned- *Young Adult Urban Fantasy/Paranormal*

(6 book series)

Book 1: Forgive Me Lucy

Book 2: Forgive Me Aiden

Book 3: Forgive Me Jena

Book 4: Forgive Me Kobe

Book 5: Forgive Me Marti

Book 6: Forgive Me Dawson

Realms Of The Fae- *Young Adult Urban Fantasy (with elements of romance)*

The Sword (short story in Like A Girl Anthology)

Heart Of Stone

Book 1: A Debt Owed

Book 2: Marked By The Hunt

Book 3: The Magic Collector

Book 4: An Unexpected Betrayal

Book 5: Imprisoned By Iron

Fairytales Retold (Short Stories)

Snow-White And Rose-Red

The Twelve Brothers

The Light Princess

Beauty And The Beast

Sleeping Beauty

Aschenputtel

The Golden Bird

The Frog Prince

The Death Of Koshchei The Deathless

Myths And Legends Retold (Short Stories)

Ion, Son Of Apollo

Sir Gawain And The Maid With The Narrow Sleeves

Princess Ilse, The Giant's Daughter

YOUNG ADULT NOVELS

Young Adult Fantasy (with elements of romance)

Elf Sight

Earth Bound

Young Adult Urban Fantasy

Stone Warrior (with elements of romance)

The Jungle Inside

Young Adult Contemporary (with elements of romance)

Through Your Eyes

The Ugly Stepsister

Perfect Little Princess

Young Adult Contemporary/Paranormal

Whispers In The Dark (with elements of romance and same sex relationships)

Over Too Soon (with elements of romance)

Young Adult Sci-Fi

Experiment X-One-Six (Urban Sci-Fi/Superheroes)

An Endless Dawn (Post Apocalyptic Sci-Fi)

CHILDREN'S BOOKS

Dragon Lord (Preteen/early teens) (Fantasy)

The Irish Wizard (Upper middle grade) (Urban Fantasy)

SHORT STORIES

Urban Fantasy

Eternally Late

Dealings With Joe

Glimpses (short story in That Moment When Anthology)

Contemporary

The Brat Next Door

Fantasy LitRPG

(Set in the same world as Guardians Of The Round Table Series)

Tales Of Inadon 1: The Disc (Co-written with Storm and Rhys Petersen) (short story in Game On! Anthology)

Post Apocalyptic Sci-Fi

Compulsive Directive

NONFICTION

A Year Of Weekly Writing Exercises (Creative Writing)

Cooking For Families With Allergies (Cooking) (Co-written with Storm Petersen)

Tell Me A Story, Grandma (Memoir)

For the most up to date details on available titles visit:

www.avrilsabine.com/books/bibliography

Assassins Of The Dead Series

To learn more about this series visit:

www.avrilsabine.com/series/aotd

BOOKS AVAILABLE IN THE SERIES

Book 1: Dark Blade

Book 2: Dragon Touched

Book 3: Society Against Vampires

Book 4: King's Request

Book 5: Duke's Courier

Disclaimer

This is a work of fiction. Names, characters, businesses, places, events and incidents are either the products of the author's imagination or used in a fictitious manner. Any resemblance to actual persons, living or dead, or actual events is purely coincidental. The opinions expressed or beliefs held are those of the characters and should not be assumed to be the opinions or beliefs of the author.

www.ingramcontent.com/pod-product-compliance
Lightning Source LLC
Chambersburg PA
CBHW020755190726
48285CB00006B/2046